SO FAIR, SO EVIL

SO FAIR, SO EVIL

PAUL CONNOLLY

CUTTING EDGE

ISBN-13: 978-1-954840-03-4

Published by
Cutting Edge Books
PO Box 8212
Calabasas, CA 91372
www.cuttingedgebooks.com

CHAPTER ONE

NOBODY KNEW how the letters came to be hacked into the side of the rock; for that matter, nobody knew how the rock itself came to be there, where for miles around there were no others bigger than a hen's egg.

Rock and letters were equally unlikely: the gray stone, man-high and twice as big around at the bottom as a wagon wheel, hulking into a bald oval from the top of which on clear days you could see for miles across the flat tilled earth to the horizon; the letters, which had appeared overnight some thirty-three years ago, without explanation and, for all anybody mortal knew, without author either, a line of foot-tall capitals wobbling halfway across the sheerest face. "REPENT," they said. If you were headed toward town you couldn't miss them.

But we were approaching from the other direction and the letters were on the far side. I punched the cab driver's shoulder.

"Stop here."

"Here?"

He looked over his shoulder with eyes startled from their half-closed bleariness. The cab slowed, rattling.

"Just for a minute," I said. "I want to open up a grave."

"You want to *what?*" The cab driver braked to a hard stop, still staring back at me.

I looked past his stubbled face and the long purple scar crawling snakelike down one side of it. The rock was at the side of the road, right by the cab's snout.

"Open up a grave," I said.

"There ain't no grave *here,* mister. Not that I ever heard tell of." A cigarette bobbed wetly between the cab driver's fat lips. The words, coming around it, were faintly pulpy.

Well, there it is, I thought, looking beyond him at the rock; just the way I remembered it. Just the way it was the night it killed her.

"Well, now, I would have sworn that was a tombstone over there," I said, nodding at it.

"What tombstone?" the cab driver said. "There ain't no tombstones here, either."

I pulled the door handle. It felt as if it would come off in my hand, but it didn't. I got out of the cab and walked around the rock. In the late afternoon, the sun was a huge red blob, turning the hot blue summer sky mellow with the slow approach of evening. Shadows from a long-leaf-pine thicket sprawled gauntly across a cotton field beside the road.

"I never heard of no tombstone," the cab driver said.

The letters were old and weather-stained, and in the late-afternoon light I could hardly read them. I knew what they said anyway. I put out my hand and touched them, first the R, then the E, with my forefinger.

Maybe right there, I thought. Maybe right there between those two letters is where her little yellow head hit and cracked wide open.

"Repent," I said, out loud.

I laughed; it was a harsh, ugly sound with no humor in it and it hurt my throat to make it. I had been laughing like that for four months, ever since I had seen the picture.

I took a step back from the rock and stared across its wide top to the cotton field and the long-leaf pines. Then I looked over my shoulder and saw the road, flat and black and narrow, bending toward the east and Old Hundred. The men who had built the first trail past there could not have removed the rock if they had wanted to, so they had curved their road around it; later builders had never seen any need to change the original roadbed or to blast the rock away, not even old Josephus Thompson, who had had to get himself elected county treasurer and threaten to call in a New York City accountant to audit the tax books before he ever got the road paved at all. That was in 1926, the year after Josephus had rebuilt Old Hundred, two miles beyond the boulder.

"Listen, mister," the cab driver said, "I got no time to waste asetting here."

I touched the letters again, then backed slowly away from the rock, still looking at it, still trying to see how it could have happened that this inert mass had killed Dolly.

"You want to go to Old Hundred or don't you?" The cab driver raced the engine impatiently.

I felt something hard and long ridged under the sole of my shoe. I moved my foot and looked down. I had been standing on a curiously shaped stone, curved and narrow, about four inches long. It was white and, in the quick-falling dusk, easily caught my eye.

"Hey," the cab driver said. "Hey, mister."

I picked up the stone. It was cool and smooth.

"I'm coming," I said. "Try to control yourself."

I looked at the curious stone, trying to feel an interest in it, trying to wonder what it was, where it had come from. I had tried to feel an interest in many things for the past four months, in many people; I had talked to people and listened to them and read about them and looked at them for hours on end, but I had not been interested in them.

"I got to get back in time to meet the seven-fifteen," the cab driver said. "How 'bout shaking it up, huh?"

I slipped the smooth white stone in my pocket and looked over my shoulder at the cab driver. I was not interested in him, either. I was interested only in Dolly. Dolly was dead. Little Dolly, with her yellow hair and her skin whiter and softer than cotton and her sad gentle eyes, was dead.

"Did you see it?" I jerked a thumb toward the rock.

He took the cigarette out of his mouth and looked at it, then threw it down hard on the blacktop road.

"See what?" he said. Did I see *what*, for God's sake?"

"The wreck. Did you see it after it happened?"

"Wreck?"

He reached over the back seat and opened the door. It screeched rustily. I moved closer to the cab, looking both ways along the road. Except for the gentle curve away from the rock, it ran almost straight for a mile in either direction.

"She was crushed," I said. "The engine came back into the front seat and crushed her."

"Oh, you mean the Sinclair girl," the cab driver said. "I'll say she was …"

He stopped and stared at me again, his big soiled hand falling slowly from the door handle.

"You Sinclair?"

"She was so *little*," I said. "It wouldn't take much to crush anybody that little, would it?"

The cab driver pulled the palm of his hand across his fat wet mouth. His glaze flicked to my face, to the long black stretch of the road, back to his steering wheel.

"This is costing you money, mister. Get in or I got to go."

"They told you I was crazy," I said. "You don't have to be nervous, though."

I went back to the rock. He doesn't have to be nervous, I thought. What does he think I'd want to do anything to him for? Why does he think I care anything about him?

I could barely see the letters now and I traced them with my hand again. "REPENT." I traced them again and they still spelled "REPENT."

All right, I thought. Dolly. Listen. I know you didn't drive that car into the rock. I'm going to make it all right for you.

4

"Mister," the cab driver said, "I ain't asking any more, I'm telling you I got to get back to town."

I swung away from the rock and went back to the car and got in. I could feel the cold white stone in my pocket and I caressed it, the enamel-like smoothness as comforting as the warm baths used to be. I wished I could take a warm bath right then.

"Old Hundred," I said.

The cab driver let the clutch in and the car jerked and moved off.

"Are you still nervous?" I said.

I could see his fat red neck stiffen. One of his shoulders moved higher than the other, as if he were waiting for a blow from behind.

"Me?" he said. "I just drive folks where they say, mister. I got no nerves."

"But I'm supposed to be crazy. They told you I was crazy, didn't they?"

"Nobody tells me nothing," the cab driver said. "If they do, I don't hear it. Me, all I want to hear is an address."

"Well, I'm glad you're not nervous. Did you really see the wreck?"

"Everybody in the county seen it."

Through the rear window, I could still see the dark mound of the rock. It was much bigger than the mound of a grave, but it had the same general shape, at that angle and distance. I closed my eyes and saw against the lids of them, like a movie in glaring color, the car crushed and hideous and, within that mangled steel, the bright glint of Dolly's hair, the broken remnants of her body.

"She took a funny way to do it," the cab driver said, "but it sure did work. It sure-God did."

"You think she killed herself? You think Dolly would have done that?"

The cab driver turned his head as if surprised.

"That's what they decided she done, ain't it?"

I let my head fall to the back of the seat and closed my eyes again. It had been one of those bright hot summer days in the South when everything shimmers, as if one were in the desert.

Maybe I ought to have gone to a hotel first, I thought. Maybe I should have got some rest.

"Nobody ever thought to see you around here again." The cab driver advanced each word cautiously, as if they were his kings in an important game of checkers. I opened my eyes and saw him watching me in the rattling rearview mirror.

"I'll bet they didn't," I said. "I'll bet they loved it when they heard I was at the nut farm, eh?"

The cab driver looked away from the mirror. He didn't answer and I closed my eyes again. I kept them closed until the cab swung into the Old Hundred drive.

Then I leaned forward, seeing in the dying light the one place in the world, besides the rock, where I had wanted to go.

"Lots of light," the cab driver said. "Big party for the holiday, I reckon."

"Holiday?"

The cab driver braked to a halt in front of the house.

"They must of really had you out of circulation, mister. Tomorrow's the Fourth of July."

"Well, I'll be damned," I said. "I forgot to buy any firecrackers."

The cab driver shook his head and reached back to open the door. I got out, pulling my suitcase behind me.

"That'll be two bucks."

I gave him two ones. He peered at them closely in the light from his dashboard, then stuck them in his shirt pocket.

"One more thing," I said.

"Yeah?" He raced his engine.

"Didn't *anybody* think it was funny that Dolly would commit suicide?"

"For Christ's sake," the cab driver said. "How should I—"

"She wouldn't have done anything like that, you see. They don't know Dolly if they think she would have."

He yanked the gear lever and the cab jumped away, its tires slipping and grinding on the gravel drive. A light from the house fell across the car and in it I could see the fat contorted face staring back at me with fear and hatred. Then the car moved on but its two taillights kept peering at me in bloodshot accusation.

He thinks I'm still crazy, I thought, watching the taillights, hearing behind me the sudden high notes of a woman laughing. He thinks I'm crazy. And maybe he's right.

I went across the short stretch of lawn between the drive and the house. To my right, I could see the flagged terrace and the tennis court beyond it. There was a swimming pool on the left but it was down a faint slope and out of sight. There was no one on the terrace or the tennis court.

The front door of the house opened and a young woman came out. It was almost dark and she didn't see me until I put my foot on the porch.

"Hello, Ann."

She was a small, trim, almost angular blonde. Her hair was pulled severely to the back of her head and her lips were unpainted. They parted in surprise when she saw me and she put a highball glass carefully down on the broad railing of the porch. I could hear the ice rattle.

"Frank. You came back."

I laughed, making that sound I had come to hate. It tasted like green bile in my throat.

"Didn't you think I would?"

"Hardly anybody did."

She moved nearer, smiling uncertainly. She picked up the glass and I thought, She does it in public now the way they always said she did in secret. She was wearing the sort of dress she had always worn—a tubular linen thing that, even outlining as it did the hard tight curves and angles of breasts and hips, made her seem as rigid as a piece of contemporary furniture.

"Well, I'm back," I said. "You can tell them I'm back." It sounded silly and vain but I hadn't meant it that way.

I put the suitcase down and looked at the great house towering above me. It had a grace, a sheer eloquence of line that, seen just right by, say, a full October moon or in a cool green spring dawn, could bring a lump of pure hurt up from somewhere inside me to my chest.

Josephus Thompson had rebuilt Old Hundred in 1926. The Thompsons had then been living on Sycamore Street, Huntsville's best residential section, since the Civil War. Josephus liked to claim that Sherman burned out the original house at Old Hundred in 1865 but, to cronies, he would admit that it had actually caught fire when his Great-Aunt Melinda dropped a hog grease candle in the attic in the starvation days of 1864, while she was looking for a trunk of old clothes to make over. Sherman came no closer than fifty miles to what was left of the place but, left alone, Josephus could make a good story out of it anyway.

Old Hundred had been a rich plantation before the Civil War, located exactly one hundred miles from the seacoast. Even after they moved to town, the Thompsons had farmed its lands with notable success. But it was not until Josephus developed a spectacular knack for trading in cotton futures and restored the family fortunes beyond even ante-bellum levels that anyone thought about rebuilding the house, the walls of which had withstood the fire.

Now, twenty-seven years after its own reconstruction, it looked exactly as it had before the war, or so Harry and Ellen Thompson, its present occupants, fondly believed. It was a two-and-a-half-storied white brick house in the classic plantation tradition, its slender columns rising past two porches to an almost flat roof, its two chimneys standing in balance at either end, its wooden blinds painted a clean bright green.

This was where Dolly had lived, where she had been brought up, I thought now, looking up at it, wondering as I had always wondered how it would have been to be a child in such a house, to be a child with all the tradition and power and privilege behind you of people who had built and. rebuilt a home like this, to be a part of a heritage that included such a place.

I hated Old Hundred. I had hated it, despite its beauty, ever since I had realized what it meant to Dolly, the power it held in her life. Now I had come back to it, but Dolly was not there, not physically, though the memory of her, for me, would lurk in every corner, beyond every door.

"Well, by God!" George Johnson said. "Where did you come from, Frank?"

He was standing beyond Ann in the doorway Josephus had had rebuilt from a description in his father's diary. George's mouth was a little open. He wore a loud checked sport shirt and I felt a real twinge of familiarity at the sight of it; George always wore loud shirts when his wife, Peggy, would let him.

"Harry!" he called. "Harry, for God's sake, *Frank's* here."

"George, you haven't changed a bit," I said.

None of them will have changed, I thought; not a one of them, damn their smug souls. They'll all be going on just the way they used to. The world hasn't changed for them. Something that made it bearable hasn't died.

I wanted to turn and run down the steps, across the lawn, after the cab. I did not want to see any of them, to have any of them dulling with their muddy talk the bright glow of my memory of Dolly. And then Harry came out on the porch. He looked a little vague and his hair needed combing.

"Frank," he said. "God, I'm glad to see you."

He put out his hand. I found in that handshake something warmer than anything I had known for a long time.

"It's time you came home," Harry said.

The warmth went out of his clasp.

"Not home," I said. "Not here, Harry."

"Hell, I know, I know. It's time you came anyway." His voice was as mellow as it had always been. He wore a faded old linen jacket and a soft shirt. His breath smelled richly of bourbon.

"I came as soon as they said I was O.K."

Harry punched my shoulder with a friendly fist. "You were O.K. all the time. It was the Navy that was all wet."

"God, you're thin," George said. "Frank, you look like hell."

"Why shouldn't he look like hell?" Harry said. "Why the hell shouldn't he look like hell?"

"It's been so long," Ann said. "How long has it been, Frank?"

"A long time," I said. "A hell of a long time."

It *was* good to see Harry. He was Dolly's half brother, and despite all the times we had differed, had even quarreled bitterly, despite his queer, other-world ways and his ignorance of mine, Harry and I had developed respect for something we sensed in each other. I looked at the clean planes of his face, at the jawline that had in it a hint of the same classic beauty I could see in his house, and I thought that it took blood and years to produce men and houses like that. I thought, too, with a bitterness so intense my cheeks sucked dryly in between my teeth, that he had been right about Dolly and me. He had been right all along.

"Where's P.B.?" Harry said. "Why isn't P.B. ever around when I want him?"

"I heah, Mistuh Harry," P.B. said. He shuffled down the porch, stooped beneath the weight of his age and his black alpaca coat. Sweat glistened on his thin lined face.

"Hello, P.B.," I said.

P.B. ducked his head and smiled, obviously frightened. "How-do, Mistuh Frank," he said. He picked up the suitcase.

"P.B. thinks I'm crazy. Did they tell you I was crazy, P.B.?"

"Now, Frank," Harry said. "P.B., you take that bag up to Mr. Frank's old room and then get Easter to fix it up for him."

P.B. hurried off, moving as swiftly as I had ever seen him move. Harry cleared his throat and George laughed uncertainly, looking from me to Harry. Ann drank from her glass, looking at me over the rim. When she took it from her pale lips, it was empty.

"Have we changed?" she said. "Do we look a lot older and different, Frank?"

I was about to answer when I heard voices from the end of the porch. They stopped abruptly. I turned slowly, knowing already who was there.

"Hello, Ellen," I said. "Peggy. How are you?"

They were in bathing suits and short terry-cloth robes, leggy young women with the high color of health and plenty of exercise and plenty of money. They stood at the end of the porch, staring at me as if I were a Hindu.

"Ellen," Harry called, "isn't it wonderful?"

Peggy Johnson pushed a hand through her short hair and looked uncertainly at Ellen, waiting for her cue. She was disheveled and wet after her swim and water dripped from her bathing suit. But Ellen was as neat and dry as Ann, who stood beside me in street clothes. Even her hair was perfectly groomed. I had never seen her when she didn't look as if a maid only moments before had put the finishing touches to her hair and her clothing and her make-up. I had never seen her with smeared lipstick or wind-blown hair or a twisted stocking seam or a rim of lace showing at the bottom of her skirt. Her whole effect was metallic, as if she were something stamped from fine alloy; but she lacked the warm depths, even, of gleaming wood.

Her eyes opened wide, narrowed again. "How long is he going to stay?" she said. She came down the porch toward us, moving with silent, efficient ease.

"Ellen!"

"He knows how I feel. He always did. You never were dumb, Frank, I always said that about you."

"I know how you feel," I said. "I know how you all feel."

She had changed least of all, I thought. She would never change. Perhaps she would not even age, would defy even time to alter her.

"You might have let Ellen know you were coming," Peggy snapped, having had her cue, her small face darting at me. "I don't think—"

"Now, pet," George said. "Now now now."

"Listen," Harry said. "Frank's tired, he must have had a long trip. Let's—"

"I'm not tired. I want to hear all about Dolly, Harry." Silence moved over the porch as tangibly as the scent of the St. Augustine grass after a rain. Ann shook her highball glass, peering into it, and the sound of the ice tinkling was as loud as a dinner bell. Harry looked at his fingernails, which needed cutting. His handsome face flushed and he shoved his hands in the pockets of his baggy seersucker trousers.

"Later," he said. "We'll have a long talk, Frank."

"There isn't anything else to tell about Dolly," Ellen said. "We wrote you everything." She had come along the porch to where we stood before the big door, above which was the fan light old Josephus had gone all the way to Alabama to buy from a man who was tearing down his house to build a filling station on the lot. "If you think we kept anything from you, it's not so."

"How about some bridge after dinner?" George said. "I haven't played with anybody that really knew the club convention since you left, Frank."

"George," Peggy said. She tugged at his arm and he looked down at her, his face turning suddenly bewildered, as it usually did when he said something that displeased her. She shook her head, her wet hair flopping about her ears.

"Or maybe you've got something to tell us," Ellen said. "Maybe that's it." Her chin tilted at me and her lips parted, showing her even, startling teeth.

"Ellen," Harry said. "Frank didn't mean anything. He and I'll have a long talk after dinner."

A long talk after dinner.

There was something—yes, that was what we had had when Dolly and I came back from Florida, married. Harry and I had had a long talk after dinner—the first of many—and Ellen had been nasty then, too, and I had laughed at her. That had not been a wise thing to do.

I looked at her shadowed face, turned now in faint exasperation toward Harry. Ellen Thompson—she had been, before marriage, old Ambassador Bullock's daughter—had always been the most beautiful woman in Huntsville. Even Dolly would admit that. The high cheekbones and arched brows and delicate nose of Ellen's face were each as regal as the whole. Looking at it, thinking of what went into the making of someone who could hold her head as proudly as Ellen did, I felt the old awe, the old fear of her come down on me like a chill. With a single glance, she had always been able to make me feel badly dressed, or as if I were using the wrong fork, or as if I had to smash my fist into someone's face.

"I won't stay long," I said.

"Now, listen," Harry said. "I'm not going to have any damned bickering before you even get your bag unpacked, Frank. Or after, either. Ellen, you try to remember your manners, and Frank, you get that chip off your shoulder." He grinned a shade anxiously. Harry could be disarming at the drop of a hat. It was part of his training as a gentleman, as master of Old Hundred.

"Amen," George said.

"You keep out of this," Peggy told him.

"O.K.," I said. "Let's have a drink on that, Harry."

"Fine." Harry took me by the arm and we went across the porch toward the door. "Don't mind Ellen," he whispered. "She gets pretty upset just thinking about Dolly."

"Harry," Peggy called, "we're coming too. Wait for us."

They were all coming. We moved through the cool dim hall with its foot-wide plank flooring and its graceful staircase vaulting toward the second floor. We went through another door and downstairs to the pine-paneled recreation room Harry had built in what had once been an underground icehouse.

While Harry mixed drinks, we sat in comfortable leather chairs and talked sporadically. Yes, I said, I was out of the—er—hospital for good. No, I didn't think I would be going back into the Navy. It *had* been a long trip to come directly to Old Hundred. Well, no, as a matter of fact, I was not quite sure what I would do now. They knew how it was, I was sure; a man wanted to know where he stood before he made up his mind. Of course he did, George said, and Peggy looked apprehensively at Ellen.

Ann sat on a cricket stool by my chair, still holding her empty glass. She smoothed her skirt carefully over her knees. "I'm glad you came back, Frank. Dolly would have wanted you to."

Somehow, I couldn't help laughing, making that same ugly rasp. Ann looked puzzled and a little shocked and stood up. Ellen and Peggy stopped whispering to each other and looked at her. George leaned on the bar, looking into a glass, and Harry fiddled with the television set in the corner, his back to us all.

I didn't want to hurt Ann. She had never been unkind to me, although, presumably, she disapproved of me as much as anyone had. We stared at each other. Her eyes were not quite clear and I wondered how many drinks she had had.

"Thanks," I said. "Thanks, Ann."

She shrugged and turned away to the bar. She touched George's arm.

"Fix me a tiny drink, George. This is a holiday, isn't it?" Her voice faintly slurred the "isn't it?"

"By golly, Frank," Harry said, turning from the TV set, "it's good to see you in condition again. Walter and Maggie'll fall all over themselves when they see you. They're coming out after dinner."

"Yes," Ellen said, "and Joe's coming too. Everybody's going to stay over the holiday. Joe will be interested to see you, Frank."

"Not any more than I will be to see him." Well, well, well, I thought. The gang's all here, then. Or will be.

"How about that bridge?" George said. "Don't forget that bridge, hey, Frank?"

Peggy stiffened. "I don't think I want to play bridge tonight, George."

I was not interested in this small snub, or in George's embarrassed silence. I sipped the bourbon and water Harry had given me. I had a hand in my pocket and I could feel the odd smooth stone I had picked up at the boulder.

Walter and Maggie and Joe, I thought. Coming tonight. That makes the whole gang of them, all right, the whole crowd that grew up with Dolly and shared her life and her time. The whole snotty bunch of them that never wanted to give her up to me. Including the one that murdered her.

CHAPTER TWO

ACCORDING TO MOST FOLKS in Huntsville, Harry Thompson could charm the birds out of the trees; but even Harry could not keep dinner that night from being dismal. He had done his best—with slight assistance from Ann—but only the appearance of Maggie and Walter Lee in the middle of the watermelon course had kept the gathering alive. Now, dinner ended, the momentary excitement of their arrival faded, Harry was still struggling; I had never seen him so near to floundering.

"Are we going to give in to those damned Reds over there, Frank?" he asked now, trying his fifth change of subject.

It seemed a long time since I had had anything to do with those damned Reds over there. I tried to think about that gray coast that had been Korea.

"That's what everyone here wants to know," George said. "Why don't we boot them back to China and get it over with?"

"Well," I said, "there are a hell of a lot of them over there. Maybe that's why."

Harry lit a cigarette with his silver lighter, nodding. George cleared his throat angrily.

"Well, ten years ago we wouldn't have put up with this kind of stuff from a bunch of Chinks. Would we, Walter?"

"You can't go by what happened ten years ago, George." Walter Lee puffed peacefully at his pipe.

Night had cooled the air and we were gathered on the flagged terrace outside the house. There were a good many stars out, even that early, and a smell of grass and wistaria and pine needles moved with the faint breeze through the night. Lights from the front porch and from a pair of French doors behind us illuminated the terrace dimly.

It was almost amusing, I thought, listening with one ear to Maggie Lee's voluble chatter—Maggie had suddenly undertaken to give me the entire history of Huntsville in the years since I had left it at the outbreak of the war in Korea, and her voice rattled on and on, with the peculiar breakneck speed that had always been to me at once her sole charm and her worst irritant, chronicling the family trivia and social oddments that had long ceased to have any meaning for me but which, to her, were the whole of history—it was almost amusing to see the different problems presented Harry by each of us.

Ellen lay in a contour chair, her long beautiful legs pointed almost upward, while the breeze toyed with the hem of the light summer dress she wore. We could not see her face and the sight of those unmoving legs and those small stiff feet in their high-heeled shoes was forbidding, as if she had symbolically removed herself from the terrace and the things being said and done there. George Johnson, restrained by Peggy from friendly overtures to me, sulked like a child and slumped in one of those folding canvas chairs in which big men look overstuffed, while Peggy herself, torn between avoiding an affront to Ellen and jibing George out of his mood, talked spasmodically and with a sort of hand-wringing gaiety to anyone, except me, who would listen—at the moment, Walter Lee, who could and would, given enough pipe tobacco, listen to anyone and even appear interested. Ann, I thought, was feeling her drinks, although she was sitting primly still and silent in a deck chair. There was something too stiff about the way she held her head, as if it were a burden her trim body could hardly carry.

Without me, there would have been no problem. I had seen too much, absorbed too much, lost too much for amiability.

That could never have happened to Harry Thompson, not even now as he struggled to keep the evening alive. He was Josephus' son, the head of the Thompson family since the old man had died, and his whole life, except during the war, had been one long lesson in the decent relationship of man to man.

The Thompsons were unquestionably Huntsville's first family. There were, of course, the Harolds and the Spencers and the Parrs and the Bullocks and the Lees and the Chapmans and the Rays, perhaps one or two other families. But none of them had produced a governor. None of their daughters had married titled Europeans. There were no Confederate generals in their backgrounds (a few colonels, perhaps, and of course there was the hero, Major Agnew Parr, whom the Yankees had hanged right on Courthouse Square in 1865). They had not consorted on familiar terms with Senators and Cabinet members and distinguished authors and at least one President.

Harry had had a carefree youth, since old Josephus gave him and Dolly, his half sister, anything they wanted. Yet he had been a serious boy, reading a lot and daydreaming and wandering over the countryside. He had once aspired to write poetry, had even had a verse or two published in some Yankee magazine; in fact, the town had not been disposed to think much of him as successor to Josephus until the war proved him a real Thompson, after all. Pearl Harbor had sent him into training as a naval aviator and his combat career in the Pacific was mildly spectacular, in every way worthy of his Civil War ancestors.

The day he came home, Josephus died; he had waited only to see Old Hundred in good hands, the town said. Dolly's mother, Harry's stepmother, had been dead for years, and Harry was the head of the first family.

He was on the platform for high-school commencements and a member of the board of directors of the Tobacco Board of Trade; the Red Cross and the March of Dimes and the Community Chest could always count on him to start the ball rolling with a generous contribution, and he had gladly accepted a place on the regional Boy Scout Council. He had organized the Community Concert Series and he had led the drive for a county hospital.

These things counted for far more than the fact that Harry's legal practice amounted to no more than a well-stocked law library; that he spent more time in his den at Old Hundred with his books and his record player and his fine old bourbon than in gainful employment; that he poured out more money each year on his show horses than most people in Huntsville earned. When the County Bar Association asked him to run for judge of the Recorder's Court, he gravely assented with the proviso that he would not actually have to campaign. The attorneys felt that he would lend such weight of prestige and dignity to the heretofore somewhat disreputable bench that they readily agreed to discourage any other candidates. Now, each Wednesday, he dispensed justice and occasional witticisms from the town's 150-year-old courtroom, for all the world like the country squire he so closely resembled.

The town chose not to notice his occasional vagueness, his failure to join the Kiwanis Club; it found something suitably democratic in his careless dress and faintly unkempt appearance; it managed to ignore the rumors that he still spent good time scribbling verses; and it thoroughly approved of his reputation as the finest horseman in the county.

"That must be Joe," Harry said.

The lights of a car had appeared at the foot of the long lawn that sloped away from the front porch of Old Hundred.

I rubbed my hands along my thighs, feeling their palms go absolutely dry.

"... so I decided to go as Mary, Queen of Scots," Maggie was saying. "You know, without my head."

The car skidded a little, coming up to the front porch, and I could hear the brakes squeal when it came to a stop. A door slammed and quick footsteps came toward the terrace.

"Walter was going to be Sir Walter Raleigh or somebody from that period and carry my head under his arm. Well, wouldn't you know that—"

"Hi, everybody!"

Joe Spencer stepped into the soft light of the terrace, waving a casual hand at Harry. "Sorry I'm late. When do the fireworks start?"

"Any minute," Ann said. "Any minute at all." She laughed, almost tipsily, but she looked perfectly prim and controlled.

Joe wore blue denim trousers and a white shirt with its sleeves rolled up. Joe never wore a tie. I had forgotten his lean dark good looks.

"Joe," Harry said, "look who's—"

"I got a couple of rockets out in the car that ought to make your hair stand right up, Harry. One of them goes off and forms a P-thirty-eight. It—"

He saw me and stopped speaking. At that moment, Ellen stood up, the folds of her white dress falling gracefully and without a sign of wrinkle about her legs, so that she looked, as always, as if she had just that instant dressed. With no more effort than that one movement, her slim figure, her proud perfect head dominated us all.

Joe thrust a hand in the pocket of his denims, looking at Ellen. She did not speak or move and he looked back at me and rocked up and forward on his toes.

"When did they let you out?" he said.

"Sorry to disappoint you, Joe. I—recovered."

Ellen had come to Joe's side; she put her hand, long and slim, tipped with a red so dark it looked almost black in the dim light, on his arm.

"Don't say anything you'll regret, Joe." Her voice was quiet and beautifully pitched, but she could not erase the ring of authority from it.

"Let him talk," I said. "Let him talk his goddamned head off."

"Oh, look here." Harry stood up too. "Isn't this all kind of—"

"I'm not going to say anything to him," Joe said. "There isn't anything to say. I'm just surprised he had the gall to come back here even if he did—recover." His jaw jutted at me like the muzzle of one of his lean hounds.

"Now listen!" Harry strode angrily into the middle of the terrace. "Let me make something perfectly clear, and that is that Frank here is my guest and welcome in my house. Anybody who isn't willing to be decent about it can leave. I mean that."

Without a word, Joe turned away. Ellen took two quick steps after him and took his arm again, stopping him. She turned back to Harry.

"Nobody's going to leave," she said. "You might remember this is my house too, Harry."

"Well, it certainly *is*," Peggy said.

"You just keep your goddamn trap shut," George said. "That's all you got to do." Peggy gasped and there was a choked snort from the corner where Walter Lee was sitting.

"He doesn't have to leave, as far as I'm concerned." I leaned back in the deck chair, ready to laugh. They were all so childish and absurd.

"This started out to be a fine holiday," Harry said. "Now we all know Frank's been through a lot and so have we. I don't see any reason we have to act like children about everything."

"Hell, no," George said.

"I'll tell you what, people." It was the first time Walter Lee had spoken since Joe had arrived. "What do you say we go out and take a look at those fireworks, especially that P-thirty-eight Joe claims he brought? Is this a holiday or isn't it?"

Maggie took my fingers in her hot moist hand. "Second the motion. Come on, Frank."

"I'll call P.B.," Harry said. "He's got everything all set up out beyond the tennis court."

He went out of the light toward the rear of the house. Ellen pulled Joe after him and George and Peggy followed. Peggy was whispering furiously to him. Ann came over to Maggie and me.

"I don't like fireworks," she said.

"Ann, dear, you haven't been drinking again, have you?" Maggie was one of those people who pride themselves on saying exactly what they think at all times—a highly overrated virtue.

"Cernly not," Ann said. She looked hurt and went out of the light by herself, moving precisely.

"We're going to have to do something about her," Maggie said. "It's really getting quite obvious."

"I didn't notice anything."

But she wasn't listening. Maggie never listened. While you were speaking, you could see her agile, impatient mind racing ahead, planning what she would say when you had finished.

We started across the terrace. Walter was just ahead. Maggie pulled at my arm with demanding hands.

"You're going to have to leave, you know." Her voice was dramatically confidential. "We'll make it hell for you here if you keep on acting badly."

We were almost out of the light; from somewhere in the dark we heard Joe laugh, suddenly and sharply. I stopped and looked down at Maggie. Her eyes were brilliantly inquisitive behind the huge horn rims she affected. They were beautiful eyes; that had to be said for Maggie. As a girl, she had been pretty, and perhaps, to some people, she still was; but she had over the years been putting on almost imperceptibly the most unpleasant kind of weight, as if she indulged secretly in too many creamed foods. She had become a little too ripe. In a year or two she would be too soft for pleasure; her flesh would be flabby under a man's fingers. I had never liked her, not even when she had made a point of befriending me, years before. I had sensed something about her as distasteful to me as the two great breasts she would press against me when we danced at the Club.

"I'll leave when I find out who killed Dolly," I said, looking into her full, soft face, watching shock widen across it, feeling her hand go tense on my arm.

"You're just being funny," she whispered. "You know you are."

But her eyes, looking up at me, were suddenly terrified, and she took her hand off my arm. Looking down at her, at the shadow that seemed to fall across her face just before we stepped into the darkness beyond the terrace, I felt the sudden terrible exultation of the executioner.

I thought of Dolly while the rockets went off against the dark sky. In their glow, I could look about me at the heads held back to watch, and find it hard to believe that hers was not among them. She had always belonged so much to Old Hundred and to these people; even, for at least a short time, to me. There was no sense, no logic, in that small bright head's not being there.

In the thin breeze I thought I could smell the scent that had hung elusively about her. Once, in the glow from a rocket, I seemed to see her little hands moving in front of my face with that peculiar, ineffable grace. In one of the bursting rockets I found the exact silvered shade of blue of her eyes.

We were sitting facing a dark expanse of the meadow where the Thompson horses took their exercise. When the rockets burst, I could see the white Kentucky fence that surrounded it. Far away, on the other side of the meadow, I could see the lights of the neat farmhouse where Mack Norton, Harry's overseer, lived with his wife and children. It was Mack's job to make Old Hundred show a profit, despite the show horses, and he did it well.

Someone knelt on the grass beside me. "Come on," Harry whispered. "This is going to go on for a long time."

I got easily to my feet, finding a pleasureless pride in the quickening responses of my muscles, which had not so long ago been useless. Another rocket went off, spreading a pale yellow glow over the lawn. Looking down, I saw Joe Spencer staring at me with his hard huntsman's eyes. There was hatred in that stare and a solid stroke of warning moved along my spine. Perhaps Joe believed me responsible for Dolly's death and hated me for it. Or was it fear instead of hate in his eyes?

I didn't know what it was, but I knew I would find out. I followed Harry toward the lights of Old Hundred. In the darkness behind me, before the next rocket went off, voices began to whisper.

Of all the men I ever knew who had dens, Harry was the only one who really had the time and inclination to use his. It was lined with bookshelves and these were stacked with the leather volumes that had come down to Harry, mostly unread, from forebears who, if less literary, still had bought only the best in books and horses. There was row after row of Keats and Dickens and Longfellow and Shakespeare and Wordsworth and Tennyson and other classics ranging far back through *Ivanhoe* and *Tom Jones* to the Greeks and Romans. One shelf was reserved for Harry's modern works, primarily those of T. S. Eliot and Ezra Pound and other poets I had never heard of as well as all the books of Dr. Douglas Southall Freeman. These, together with the *Progressive Farmer* and the *Virginia Quarterly Review* and the university *Law Journal,* formed the bulk of Harry's reading. I had never known him to read a contemporary novel, although Dolly had told me he had read *So Red the Rose.*

It was a dark room; the furniture was massive and aged and the walls seemed to converge near the ceiling. Harry's console record player was against one wall and above it there were special shelves for the vast record collection he had made, mostly of chamber music, grand opera and chorales.

A dark portrait of Josephus over Harry's desk glared down at the room as if the old man fundamentally disapproved of such places; and he had. Dolly had told me he had never used it, had wanted to make it into a gun room.

Harry sat down behind a broad desk on which a game of ping-pong could have been played and motioned me into a leather chair across from him. I sat down and gave his huge globe a twirl, then stopped it with my finger. I had put it squarely on Capetown, South Africa, which meant nothing to me.

"Damn it," Harry said, "you have to expect a little bit of what they're giving you, walking in here the way you did."

"All right. I'm not complaining about anybody's manners."

"They're my friends, though. I don't want to lose them either."

I gave the globe another twirl and put my head back and tried to stare down old Josephus and couldn't. I was damned glad he had been dead and gone before my time in Huntsville, if this painting looked anything at all like him.

"You want me to go. Is that it?"

Harry took a cigarette out of his pack and tossed the pack to me.

"I quit smoking," I said, and tossed it back on his desk. "I don't do a lot of things I used to do."

He lit the cigarette, looking at me for a moment through the first blue haze of the smoke.

"You stay as long as you want to," he said. "The hell with them."

I put my finger out and stopped the globe again; this time I had landed near Hobart, Tasmania. I looked at the globe carefully and for a long time because his words had moved me, strangely, and I didn't want to show it. Harry was all right; he was a little stuffy and he thought too much about how things would look, but when the chips were down he was all right.

"It's a long time since I've seen you," Harry said.

Something was wrong in the room. Something was missing. I stared at the antique clock on the mantel above the old-fashioned fireplace. Nine o'clock, it said. But what ...

"Lot of water under the bridge."

"A hell of a lot." Then I discovered what it was. "What happened to your china dog?" I said. I pointed at the bare spot on the mantel where he had always kept it.

He drew on his cigarette. "Oh, Easter finally managed to break it cleaning up. Practically broke our hearts at the same time."

Once, while they were courting, Harry and Ellen had gone to a carnival that played Huntsville and she had won a china dog for popping balloons with darts. It must have meant something to them both, for they had kept the ugly white prize proudly on display. The dog was a heavy and graceless object, almost vulgar with its fatuously grinning St. Bernard's head and its long slender pointer's tail, but I missed seeing it on the mantel. It had always seemed to narrow the gap between me and Old Hundred. Not that anything could really do that.

"Tell me about Dolly, Harry."

"I still can't believe it, Frank. I never would have thought Dolly would do such a thing. Even if she had any reason."

"No," I said. "Not Dolly."

"But there doesn't seem to be any doubt." He hitched forward in the deep leather desk chair and told me about the night Dolly died. I had had the facts in a long letter from him, but this was different.

For days, he said, Dolly had been moody and, if not unhappy, at least a bit depressed. But nobody had thought much of it. Dolly was a moody girl, I would remember that. For a person who could be so sunny and cheerful, she could be awfully queer and silent sometimes. She had always been that way, even as a child.

Well, Harry said, he and Ellen thought little of her mood this time. Maybe she was blue about my being way over in Korea and no chance of getting home any time soon. Maybe a lot of things.

So at first they refused to believe it when Sheriff Charlie Stoneman woke them up at five o'clock on the morning of June the eighteenth, a year ago, and told them Dolly was dead and that it looked like suicide. But there in Dolly's room—I would remember that she had closed up the apartment she and I had had in town and had moved back out to Old Hundred—they found a note that pretty well clinched it.

Dear Frank:
    You know I can't go on this way. Or did you know that when it all started? I can't believe that but I can't believe it will ever change either.

"I sent that note along with the other stuff to the hospital, Frank. Did they ever give it to you?"

"They gave it to me," I said. "Go on."

Harry's voice was low and unemotional but I knew how close he and Dolly had been, how sometimes they had seemed more like close devoted friends than half brother and sister. It was easy to see how he suffered, telling me about the way she had died.

She had been out riding that night in the green Jaguar she had bought for herself, he said. She often did that and he and Ellen had not given it a second thought, not even when they went to bed at twelve and saw that she was not home yet. Later they learned that she had seen Ann Harold, that the two had ridden out to Steve's Place—that was a new drive-in, I wouldn't remember it, but everybody went there now—and that she had dropped Ann off at the Harold home at about eleven-thirty. That was the end of the trail until an old Negro, going to town with produce early the next morning, had found the green Jaguar wrecked against that big boulder down the road a piece—the one that had "Repent" chipped on it—with Dolly dead and crushed inside.

What made Sheriff Stoneman call it suicide right away, Harry said—his voice dropping to a whisper, full of pain and recollected shock, so that I had to lean forward to hear it—was that he could see by the car tracks, which were plain because it had rained the night before and the shoulder was softer than usual, that Dolly had driven the Jaguar right up to the rock from the direction of Old Hundred, parked it with the left wheels off the blacktop, sat there for a long time, then backed up, with the left wheels still off the road, and driven straight ahead, at what must have been at the final moment a terrific speed, into the boulder.

That was the worst thing of all to him, Harry said. He could hardly bear to think of her sitting there looking at the big boulder and thinking of doing it and then backing off very carefully and taking aim and killing herself. Even now, he said, it ripped the heart out of him just to think about it.

There was silence in the room when he had finished. The rockets were going up on the other side of the house, and although we could not see their light, the dull boom of the explosions would occasionally reach us. There were cricket and bullfrog noises, too, but most of all there was silence, a silence like water under a microscope: full of small wiggling things.

He had re-created for us both a being in which we had invested much of our lives. He had brought Dolly back to that room, and when he had finished, for a long time we sat alone with her, he with his version and I with mine, a version of Dolly that, in my case, was forever bright and tiny and sad, as if her quick smile had been a screen for some secret failure.

"Just to think of her doing that. It rips the heart out of me, Frank."

I said it ripped the heart out of me, too; and then I told him something I had sworn to a rock and a ghost that I would prove:

"She didn't do it," I said. "Anyone who says she did doesn't know Dolly the way I knew her."

He sat up in his chair, moving slowly, another cigarette clamped between his lips. I did not think he was surprised.

"Do you think I want to believe it? Do you think it's easy for me, either? But that note didn't lie, Frank. It was typed on her typewriter, right there on the desk in her room. And those tracks didn't lie, either. I tell you, Stoneman took me out there and he had it all roped off. God, it was awful. There must have been a thousand people jammed around, every lousy Tom, Dick, and Harry in the county trying to get a look at Dolly lying there. And you could look at those tracks and it was like reading her mind. It was like watching her *think* about it and then not being able to do a thing while you actually saw her do it."

"*Why,* though? Why would Dolly do that?"

He closed his eyes.

"I keep remembering her mother, Frank. Dolly's mother was ... a weakling, I suppose. I never knew why Father married her. She wasn't right for the Thompsons, she didn't belong at Old Hundred. She was a mousy, bloodless ... nothing. Maybe ... She was Dolly's mother, Frank. I despised her, but maybe there was ... something of her in Dolly."

"Maybe so," I said. "But Dolly didn't kill herself."

He stood up and leaned forward, his knuckles rapping down hard on the glass top of his desk.

"Is that why you came back?"

I gave the globe another spin. I had put my other hand in my pocket and my fingers caressed the smooth stone I had picked up where Dolly died.

"I lived and worked in this town, Harry. My wife is buried here. I even maybe have one or two friends scattered around. I had a right to come back, no matter what I thought."

Harry sat down again. I stopped the globe and this time my finger poked right down on the East China Sea. That was more like it; that had some meaning for me, not like Hobart, Tasmania.

"You came back here in the face of that note, Frank. You came back here knowing how this town felt about Dolly. You must know everybody thinks she did it because of you."

I laughed, making that same harsh sound I had been making since the day, two months earlier at the Philadelphia Naval Hospital, I had looked at a photograph I wasn't supposed to see and immediately opened my mouth and started to speak again, in a voice creaking from disuse.

"Do *you* think she did it because of me?"

"I don't *care* why she did it, Frank. I know you never meant it that way if she did."

It was my turn to stand up now. I looked down at him, safe and solid behind his huge desk, big and well fed and handsome and a trifle unkempt. Here was everything, in one man, that I had never had: wealth and security and confidence and poise and a position so impeccable it maintained itself, did not even need the crutch of precise dress. Here was what Dolly had also had and what she had had a right to expect from her husband.

Old Josephus glared down at us. I was pretty sure he would not have had me in the house if he could have had any say in the matter. I glanced at him, my eyes going up past the sound, conservative check of Harry's sport shirt and the clean classic outline of his chin and jaw and the poised glance of his eyes, until my own gaze locked with that of the fierce old man in the painting, who, more than even Harry Thompson, represented all the things I had not had for Dolly, all the things I would never have for anybody.

My knees began to tremble. The room went soft and wavy, as if seen through a rain-splashed window pane. I had dreaded this moment. I had known it was coming because I had experienced it before, in the last days at the hospital, once in the men's room of the train: this moment when my brain would begin to split open, when the pain would slash down through reason and emotion and conscience to something beyond.

"Frank?" Harry said. "Frank, are you all right?"

In that retreat, that agonizing slide away from reality, I saw his face blown up twice life size and distorted, like a face on a balloon a child buys at the county fair. I saw beside it the old man's face, too, just as large, just as distorted, glaring at me like a gigantic and disapproving juror. And between them was

Dolly—not oversize, not twisted, her bright delicate face turning slowly and proudly and gracefully from one to the other of them.

"Frank?"

I had taken her from between those two giant guardian heads, I had taken her from the place where she belonged, and I knew—perhaps Harry didn't, perhaps she had kept that secret, had let it die with her—I knew what it had done to her.

Were they right, then? Was Dolly a suicide and was I to blame? "Or did you know that when it all started?" the note had said.

Harry seized my arm and shook it roughly. The faces began to recede, grew smaller and less distorted. He shook my arm again and I watched them pop one by one into nowhere, like bubbles from a soap pipe.

"I'm all right," I said. "I just felt a little funny for a minute."

"Christ, Frank, you looked awful. You looked like you'd seen a..."

He stopped, embarrassed, and I laughed, making that same horrible sound. I wished I could make some other.

"Maybe I did," I said. "Maybe I did."

CHAPTER THREE

ALL THE ROCKETS had been fired when I got back to the sloping lawn above the tennis court. It was pitch-dark and much cooler; a cloud had come in from the west, blackening the sky and dampening the air.

I walked across Harry's St. Augustine grass toward the Belgian turf of his tennis court. A flashlight stabbed irregularly into the darkness beyond the court and I went incuriously and, on the damp grass, noiselessly toward it.

It was P.B., picking up the rocket shafts left from the fireworks display, his thin old body bending gruntingly to a job he could as easily have left for daylight.

"Hello, P.B.," I said.

He jerked upright and took two steps backward.

"Who dat?"

"Me. Frank Sinclair."

The flashlight flicked on, wavered, went out, showing briefly a pair of incredibly small feet moving nervously on the damp grass.

"You can leave that till morning," I said.

"Miss Ellen she say—"

"Never mind Miss Ellen," I said. "You do what I say."

The dark shadow of P.B. went rapidly away from me across the lawn toward the house.

"Yassuh!"

The ancient voice, thinned and bloodless with age and dedication, quivered with the abject fear his race and generation had of the abnormal. I watched him go, thinking of all the times he had, with his unquenchable belief in my commonness and bad origins, slighted and ignored and belittled me from the safe citadel of his attachment to the "fambly." I had had to go to a mental hospital to rate any respect from P.B.

I went across the thick grass to the tennis court. Beyond it, the house gleamed dully, as if gauze cut the glare of its lights. Everyone else was at the swimming pool, far out of earshot on the other side of the house. It was very quiet there on the lawn, quiet and dark and somehow deep, as if the opaque sky were the surface of an infinite lake.

I went around the wire backstop of the tennis court, stepping carefully on the imported turf so my leather heels would not cut it. The white lime of the back line was the faintest of gleams in the darkness and I could not see the net at all. At mid-court it loomed up in front of me and I put my hand on it and walked to the side lines.

"Hello," Ann said. I looked up and saw the crimson glow of her cigarette where she sat in the elevated umpire's chair.

"Why aren't you in swimming?"

"I've got on my suit," she said. "But all of a sudden I felt a little woozy and I came down here to let it wear off." The cigarette arched out in a crimson trajectory over the tennis court.

"You ought not to throw cigarettes on Harry's expensive grass."

"I know it."

I put my hand on the step of the umpire's chair beside my shoulder and leaned on it, looking up. I could see the shape of her, sharp and rigid and somehow appealing against the sky, which was being lightened by the imminent coming of the moon. Inches from my face, I could make out the shape of her ankle and bare foot.

"You know," she said, "Dolly was the only one in this whole town I really cared about."

I didn't say anything. The foot jerked, as if all its owner's muscles had tensed.

"Frank, why did she kill herself?"

"I don't know."

"You ought not to have married her, Frank."

I clenched my hands together and began to squeeze, as hard as I could.

"I told her it wouldn't ever work, no matter how nice a guy you were."

My knuckles began to pop. I squeezed my hands harder.

"But she was so determined. She was always that way, Dolly was; she was little and delicate, but she was tough. She knew what she wanted."

"No, no," I said, the unbidden words pulled out of me by a hand I could no more resist than, years ago, I could resist the melting appeal in Dolly's great blue eyes, in her childishly quivering lips. "No, that's just it, she *didn't* know what she wanted, Ann, she could never find *something* she was always looking for. That was what people never understood about Dolly, that with all she had she never had what she wanted."

"What was that?" Ann said. "What was it Dolly wanted, then?"

How can you know what somebody wants? I thought. What good does it do to ask *me* what Dolly wanted? Or anybody else?

"I don't know. But I don't think she found it in me."

A light came on somewhere on the second floor of the house and dropped a long slanting spear of yellow across the lawn, pointing like a finger to the dark tennis court. I could hear someone begin to play the Steinway that Ellen claimed Paderewski had played on one of his early tours, before she and Harry bought it from a destitute old gentleman in Warrenton, Virginia. It was Peggy playing, doing the one thing she could do all on her own, even if not very well. She was playing "Night and Day" and the sound of it took me far back, to many another night at Old Hundred, with Peggy insistently at the piano.

"Poor Frank," Ann said. "Dolly's dead but you're still alive. It's all over for her but not for you, is it?"

"Maybe it is."

"Maybe you're right. Maybe it was all over for both of you the night you met her."

The insistent piano poured its notes down the night; they flowed ceaselessly over her words and they caught me like a great tide and tumbled me frantically into the past, the words crashing on my head like breakers:

"... all over for both of you the night you met ..."

Every night when I first came to town, I walked for hours along Huntsville's dark shrub-smelling residential streets, murmurous with the slow laughing voices from the broad porches beyond the inevitable wide lawns dotted with their stone bird baths. I was young and hopeful; it seemed quite possible, then, that someday I might own one of those broad porches, too, and one of those great sweeps of lawn.

One night, a short distance ahead of me, I saw a girl getting out of a small foreign car stopped at the curb. The street light glinted from her yellow hair. I knew Dolly Thompson at once. While I walked toward her she stared at me as if I were an enemy. When I reached her she stamped her little foot on the pavement.

"It won't *start!*" she said, as if I were to blame.

"It won't?" I was not much of a conversationalist.

"*Try* to fix it," she said. "Please try."

When I had seen her before, always at a distance, she had been hurrying. Once she had even been running across the green square that enclosed the ugly old courthouse, and she had seemed to me then like a flighty little pet someone had let loose, who had found the world too large and too frightening and who was running in search of its owner.

But I could look down now into those blue eyes that even in the dark sparkled in some special way, and I thought as I stared into that white and pleading face that here was more than mere beauty. Here, somehow disclosed in the tilted nose and the tremulous dark bow of her mouth and the line of jaw and chin so delicate I would have been afraid to trace it with my forefinger— here was a creature capable not only of inducing ecstasy, but of experiencing it as well.

"You *will* fix my car, won't you?"

I would gladly have died trying, but just then she swayed toward me. I smelled whisky on her breath and she put her forehead against my chest. Her knees began to give way and her head and shoulders slid gently down my body before I caught her arms. Dolly Thompson was drunk.

I caught her, picked her up—she was weightless, as if her slim little body had no earthly substance—and, opening the front door of the little car, tucked her in. I ran around to the other side and got in behind the wheel, drawing my long legs up around my chin.

The key was not in the ignition; presumably that explained why the car would not start. I searched through her handbag and found the key and started the engine right away.

I drove rapidly out the road toward Old Hundred. When I swung into the drive, she still had not stirred. I pulled up in front of the great white house, careful to make no brake or gear noises. Her yellow hair, worn short, framed her little face softly and with a youthful effect. I could easily have imagined she was a child, asleep after a long hard day. But my foot kicked something hard on the floor of the car; it rolled across and hit the door and I knew it was a whisky bottle.

"Miss Thompson," I whispered, touching her arm tentatively. "You're home."

"I know it," she said in a perfectly normal voice. "I can smell the sweet shrub."

She opened her eyes. I was leaning all the way over her and her face was vertically under mine. It was my first experience not only with her amazing resiliency, but with the innocently magnetic quality of her face in repose, which, I would come to know later, made it impossible to look at her asleep or with her eyes closed without bending closer and closer until at last you could feel the warm feather touch of her breath on your lips and cheeks.

"You're big," she said. "Real big. What's your name?"

"Frank Sinclair."

She seemed hardly to lift her head at all, but her lips, cool and soft and tasting faintly of cherries, brushed across mine as lightly as, a moment before, her breath had touched me.

"Thank you," she said. "You're real nice, too."

She would not let me walk home, as I at first insisted; and so I had my first encounter with the pursed disapproving lips of P.B., who, roused from his sleep, grudgingly called a taxi while Dolly, apparently totally sobered by her short ride home, sat on the porch and talked to me about a new evening dress she had ordered from Lord and Taylor's.

It was not until nearly a month later, after we were married, that I found out Joe Spencer had been passed out cold in the back seat of the little foreign car and that he had spent the entire night there, completely forgotten by Dolly, and that when he awoke the next morning he let the air out of the tires, in a spirit of pure revenge, before riding one of Harry's Tennessee walking horses to town bareback.

I suppose Joe was more bewildered by the events of the next few weeks than anyone in Huntsville except me. But I was in love and I never noticed him; I was too busy with Dolly.

I saw her every night. We danced at roadhouses and went for long rides in the country in the ridiculous little car and swam in the pool at Old Hundred under the disapproving eyes of P.B., who brought us tall cool drinks on a silver tray. We went on picnic trips to the beach and a fishing trip down along the black deep slow river that wound through a swamp twenty miles away.

"This isn't me," I told her once. "This isn't really Frank Sinclair at all."

"It looks like you. I could have sworn it was you."

We had made a one-day trip to the beach and I lay propped on my elbows on an old Army blanket, looking down at her face, the tender skin of which seemed not even to notice the broiling sun.

"But it can't be me, Dolly. The real Frank ... if you knew him, you wouldn't give him the time of day."

"He's a slob," she said. She reached up and removed my sunglasses. Her arm darted suddenly at me, slid smoothly around my neck. She was amazingly strong for so small a girl, and she bent my head swiftly until her lips were touching my ear.

"Whoever it is," she said, "whoever you are, kiss me."

Oh, I was happy in those bright kaleidoscopic days that were summed up in an image I had of Dolly coming running down the lawn of Old Hundred, her yellow hair flouncing lightly at each step and her small beautiful head flung back and one arm reaching out eagerly toward me. I was happy even when I found her looking at me with her exquisite brows drawn together and her small white teeth pinching her lower lip and an expression in her eyes that I could hardly bear: a sadness that seemed to flow through her hands or her lips or her wind-blown hair into me, until the compact world we inhabited together was drenched with it, with that rich sweet sadness that was like the sound of a cello. I sensed it even in her gayest moments—and nobody could be gayer than Dolly; nobody could laugh so musically and with such complete abandonment to whatever joy, whatever happiness was handy; nobody could find such pure fun in so little.

But it bothered me only momentarily. In the time there was for wonder, I wondered at the unbelievable truth that this was

Dolly Thompson in my arms, that these were her fragile hands on mine, that these were her lips, still tasting of cherries.

Huntsville wondered too and talked and did not hesitate to point. I was aware of its amazement and its disapproval and, faintly, of some of its outrage. I couldn't help knowing the town would never consider me good enough for Dolly.

The Atlantic Power and Light Company had sent me there, as branch engineer. This position automatically entitled me to an honorable spot in Huntsville's business life, as well as to company-paid memberships in Rotary, the Jaycees, the Tobacco Board of Trade, and several other organizations to which I did not want to belong.

But I had learned my trade through the company's own training program and from a four-year World War II hitch as a naval officer specializing in electronic mine devices, not through one of the two or three colleges Huntsville regarded as nonsubversive, God-fearing, and socially acceptable. I was a stranger from a mill town that had not even been in existence when Sherman passed through going north. And, out of the sheer love of it, I put in as much time at manual labor, side by side with my line crews, as I did behind my desk.

Such a man found no Huntsville dowagers asking him to tea, received no invitations to Sunday dinner on Sycamore Street.

There was, above all, no disposition to match me with Dolly Thompson. And after the night we rode across the state line and were married by a justice of the peace who also sold white whisky in quart Mason jars, it was, to the people of Huntsville, as if the courthouse in whose shadow they had grown to maturity had burned down; as if the Baptist minister, after thirty-four years, had accepted a call to another congregation; as if someone had opened a brothel in one of the tall ugly houses on Sycamore Street.

Dolly Thompson, who had been beauty queen at Flora Scott College, who had led the Cotillion Club ball at Capital City, who had turned down an offer to be in a Woodbury's Soap ad, who could have had anybody—just *anybody*—had married a stranger, a man who was little more than a workman, whose father—so it was correctly rumored—had been a comber in a textile mill.

"By God," Harry shouted at me a week later, the night we came back to Old Hundred, "by God, Sinclair, do you think anybody in this town is going to take you in and shake your hand for this?"

"Don't be mad at Harry," Dolly whispered to me later that night from the depths of the old feather mattress of her canopied bed in one of Old Hundred's stately bedrooms. "He'll be for us in the long run. You'll see. Harry will be for anything I want."

And he was. But all that was later, and in the middle of the shock and outrage and amazement we had caused, it was P.B. that had the last word:

"You done blistered yoah tail," he said to Dolly—Dolly sitting tiny and calm in the vast formal living room of Old Hundred while Harry shouted at me in the den, Dolly sitting there unflinching under the chiseled icy disapproval of Ellen—"like yoah pa done when he maa'd yoah ma. You done blistered yoah tail and now you got to sit on it."

Abruptly, as if someone had seized her wrists, Peggy stopped playing. Another light came on on the second floor, flinging out a second yellow finger, as accusing as the first, toward the tennis court. I heard the click of a cigarette lighter in the umpire's chair above my head.

"I loved her, Ann. God knows I loved her."

"You always did think that ought to make up for all the rest."

"You saw her that night, didn't you? The night it happened?"

"We had a hamburger and a Coke together. She was depressed."

"What about?"

"Nothing. I don't know. You know how Dolly was. She was always..."

"Did she say anything about me?"

"She said she'd had a letter from you."

"This is like pulling teeth," I said.

"I don't *remember* much she said. Mostly she talked to Joe. She didn't—"

She gasped, as if trying to jerk the words back into her throat. The foot and ankle moved and she stood up. I moved in front of the umpire's chair and seized both her ankles, squeezing hard.

"Joe," I said. "Tell me about Joe being with her that night."

"Take your hands off me, Frank Sinclair!"

"Not till you tell me about Joe and Dolly."

"There's nothing to tell."

"It just slipped out, didn't it? It just slipped out that he was with her that night, even if you didn't mention anything like that to the police."

"Listen." Her whisper was as dryly fierce as a jet of steam. "You know what would happen if I screamed? If I say you... attacked me?"

Fear was sobering, and there was nothing at all spurious about the threat in her words. Ann Harold could be deceptive in many ways, I knew that; but I had to believe, knowing her, that she would do what she threatened.

She was the last bearer of a name as proud as any in Huntsville. Her only brother had been killed at Omaha Beach; on the same day, most folks thought, her father died too, although his mortal shell lingered, breathing asthmatically, for another two years.

Now, nine years after Billy Harold had jumped from his assault craft onto the beach that, moments later, would be not only his graveyard but that of his name and seed, it looked as if there would not even be Harold blood in some youngster of a different name; it looked as if the blood itself would end with Ann.

Since Billy's death, she had pointedly discouraged the few men who had shown interest in her severe good looks. She devoted her time to church and woman's club and charitable work, as her mother had done before her. She allowed herself little social life, though she had as many invitations and opportunities as Huntsville afforded.

But sometimes, for days, she would disappear into the tall ugly old Harold home on Sycamore Street, tended only by an old colored woman who would refuse admittance even to the Episcopal rector. It was a fairly open secret that on those occasions Ann Harold went to bed with several bottles and stayed there until she chose to end her alcoholic retreat. Her grandfather, the town loved to point out, had done the same sort of thing half a century before.

On the whole, though, Huntsville chose to overlook this weakness. Usually, with that queerly effective unanimity of small satisfied towns, it forbore even to mention it.

"Oh, Ann," Dolly used to say. "All Ann needs is a man."

I didn't know about that; but I knew I was taking no chances with her. I let go of her ankles.

"If I screamed, they'd send you back to Philadelphia so fast—"

"All right," I said. "I know they would. If that's the way you want it, go on and scream."

"That's not the way I want it."

"All right," I said. "All right."

There was a long silence. In the middle of it, Peggy started playing again. This time she played what she called "Chopin," but what was really only a popularized version of a polonaise. She played it with an odd flair and, standing there on the dark tennis court listening to the martial notes, I wondered if, given not just opportunity but also motive, Peggy might not really have been able to play Chopin or anything else. You never could tell what people were capable of, not even Peggy.

"It's nothing you could go to the police about, anyway. Not now."

"Maybe not."

"It's just Joe I keep thinking of."

"It's just Dolly *I* keep thinking of," I said. I knew she was going to tell me, then.

"George," I heard Peggy call behind me. She had stopped playing. "*Geor*-orge?"

"We were parked out at Steve's Place," Ann said, "having a hamburger and a Coke. She was telling me about this letter from you and how horrible the war sounded the way you told about it. Then Joe's car pulled up beside us and he came over and got in with us. I was in the middle but they both leaned around me, sort of leaving me out, I guess.

"I was only half paying attention. It was June and I was thinking about all the little girls getting married and all the weddings I'd been in. But I remember Joe saying something about her going down to the beach that week end and I remember her saying in that vague way she had, as if she didn't quite have her mind on what she was saying, 'But why in the world should I do a thing like that?'"

"George!" Peggy's voice was sharper and louder behind us.

They had left Joe's car at Steve's, Ann said—it was so long ago, a year now, she was not clear why they had done this—and driven back into Huntsville in the Jaguar. It was quite late, she thought, almost midnight, and the streets were deserted. They had driven to Ann's and Joe had walked with her across the wide lawn to the great empty dark house. Then Ann had sat on the front porch smoking a final cigarette, watching them drive off, still thinking about all the June brides she had known and wondering vaguely if Dolly had been spending week ends with Joe, if her answer about the beach trip had been just a blind.

"But Joe swears there was never anything like that. He called the next morning and told me what...what Dolly had done.

I couldn't believe it. Dolly was such a *private* creature, she was so gentle. I could feature her maybe, if things were bad enough, doing something secret, like drowning herself with weights so she wouldn't come up again and nobody would ever see her, but...but..."

"You couldn't feature Dolly making such a mess, such ugliness, could you?"

"Maybe that's it. Anyway, Joe had to practically shout at me to get me to realize what he was saying. I guess I went to pieces. I was standing there crying and trying to hang up and he kept asking me something and asking me and I said, 'Yes, yes, all right, Joe....' I would have said anything just to get rid of him. Later I realized I'd agreed not to mention that he'd seen her the night before. He said that was one thing we could do for her, keep any talk like that from starting."

I stepped back from the umpire's chair.

"Come on down," I said.

One of the second-story lights went out, but just then the moon edged from behind the cheeselike cloud moving eastward. It spread an amber glow over the tennis court.

She stood up; she was wearing a long white robe over her bathing suit. She came down the three vertical steps facing me. As she reached the last one I put my hands under her arms and picked her off the step and put her on the ground. One of my hands went inside the white robe and brushed across the Lastex edging of her bathing suit and the bare slope of her breasts. She jerked away as if I had touched her with ice.

But it had been over a year since I had touched a woman. The smooth softness my fingers had brushed sent a jolt like an electric shock all through me and I wrestled her closer, my mouth going dry and my hands meeting at the small of her arched back.

"Frank...don't...Frank!"

Her breasts against me were hard and unyielding. Her whole body was rigid as a fence post, and as I bent my head toward her, her fingers clutched, yanked at my hair.

"George!" Peggy's voice, shriller now, came through the darkness again.

I lifted my head. Her fingers ripped once more at my hair and I pushed her away.

"Ann … listen, I didn't mean …"

Her breath was harsh and fast in her throat, as if she had run a long distance.

"Ann," I said. "I'm sorry. Please … forget it, will you?"

She shrank back against the umpire's chair. Christ, I thought, this goddamn town hasn't treated you any better than it has me.

There was nothing else I could say, even if she would have listened. I turned away. The meadow beyond us and the lawn stretching up the hill past the tennis court to the house were silent now, and I could hear the faint ghostly slither of the first evening breeze. Peggy must have found George, for she had stopped calling him.

CHAPTER FOUR

WENT IN through wide French doors to the formal living room of Old Hundred. The great piano's mahogany gleamed dully in the light from a brass floor lamp. In one corner there was a three-sided cupboard full of old china Harry's great-grandmother or somebody had painted with fragile pastel flowers. There was a small fireplace, closed for the summer with a wrought-metal cover, beneath a fluted mantel.

That room represented wealth. Its antique furniture, the old cut glass in another cabinet beyond the piano, the thick rug underfoot—all these things were silent tributes to the vast power of the Thompson name. I wondered, as I had so often, what you could do with such power, how you could be sure of wielding it equitably even if you wanted to.

In the great hall, with its graceful stairs, the wide planks of the flooring were smooth and polished under my feet. My wet shoe soles crunched uncomfortably.

The door to Harry's den was ajar. I pushed it open without knocking and walked in. The room smelled strongly of tobacco and whisky. In the small brilliant circle of light from the desk lamp I could see Harry, one leg resting up on the desk. Walter Lee stood in shadow by the window, his pipe in his mouth, his hands thrust down into the pockets of the nondescript khaki trousers he usually wore after office hours. Joe sat in the same leather chair I had occupied earlier in the evening, twirling the globe with an extended forefinger, just as I had done.

"Come on in, Frank." Harry took his leg down from the desk. "How about a drink?"

"Sure. I'll fix it."

I went to the sideboard where Harry kept his liquor and a bowl of ice cubes.

"We were just talking about this new plastics plant they're building over at Marion," Harry said. "Have you heard about that, Frank?"

I poured bourbon into a glass and dropped two ice cubes in after it. From the corner of my eye I could see Joe looking at the tips of his battered loafers; his lips were set more tightly than usual.

"I've been a little out of touch, Harry."

"It sounded like Maggie was giving you a complete newsreel tonight," Walter said. He chuckled.

"She didn't mention a plastics plant, though."

"Say," Harry said, "I just thought, I advised them on the real estate when they decided to go in over there and I know some of their top management. Have you made up your mind what you're going to do yet, Frank?"

"I want to look around a while."

"Well, they ought to be able to use a trained engineer. Want me to make a phone call or two for you?"

I poured plain water from a glass pitcher over my bourbon and ice, set the pitcher down, and swirled the ice cubes around with my finger; then I turned and took a step toward the three of them waiting inside the white circle of light. The empty place on the mantel, where the china dog had been, caught my eye. Joe's knees were crossed and just by my leg one of his loafers pointed stiffly.

"I appreciate it," I said. "Maybe later. Just now, things are too much up in the air for me to decide."

"Jesus Christ," Joe said. "If I ever heard of somebody looking a gift horse in the mouth, that's it."

I looked down at his shoe. Its sole was worn thin and a hole was beginning to break through. It was typical of Joe to have a hole in his shoe. He had probably never had as much money, all at one time, in his life as Ellen Thompson would pay for a new fall wardrobe. He worked as an auto salesman for the Dixie Motor Company, but no harder or more often than was necessary to pay the taxes on his high old Sycamore Street house and to buy a minimum of clothes and food for his mother and himself and his hounds.

Joe Spencer was the only man in Huntsville who had killed a wild boar or caught a marlin. His clothes were threadbare and his house was unpainted, but he had the best pair of foxhounds in the eastern part of the state, a couple of fine shotguns and two rifles, a ramshackle motor launch at Shirley's Inlet, and a trunkful of spliced and mended fishing gear. His great-grandfather had been killed a hero at the Bloody Angle and his grandfather had been in Congress for thirty-two years and his father had died a jovial alcoholic; from them, he had left only his name and his lean dark good looks and his thin strong hands that caressed a shotgun as if it were a woman. With only those assets he might still have had his pick of Huntsville's most eligible girls; but he had never given a damn for any of them.

No, I thought, staring down at the scuffed toe of his loafer, only for Dolly. Only for my wife. There was a slow tightening in my chest. I was squeezing the long smooth stone in my pocket.

"Gift horses are one thing," I said. "Another man's wife is something else."

The loafer jerked out of my sight. I put the glass to my lips and drank half the highball, not looking at any of them.

"What the hell is that supposed to mean?" Joe said.

Harry stood up. "Now, don't you two start …"

"We're not *starting* anything, Harry. Are we, Joe?"

"No. It started a long time ago."

"Listen, let's all have another drink. Why don't we—"

"Why don't we let them talk it out?" Walter said. His voice was quiet, almost casual.

"When I married Dolly," I said. "Isn't that when it started?"

Joe put his head back and laughed. He laughed quite loudly and for a long time. There was derision in the sound of it, and contempt too. It was a sound only a Spencer or a Thompson—their kind—could have made, I thought, the sort of reckless laughter of which only men like Harry and Joe were capable. I had seen them race once in an impromptu steeplechase Harry had staged in his meadow; in the way they sat their horses, in the way their heads flung back out of what seemed to me pure physical joy in action, in speed, in dominance of the huge animals under them, I had found something reminiscent of their ancestors, of those fierce older Thompsons and Spencers who had ridden out to war in gray uniforms and on such horses as these and with just such handsome laughing flung-back heads.

Joe's laugh died slowly. I looked up at the portrait of old Josephus. It wasn't laughing, but it looked less disapproving now that someone had put me in my place.

Joe said, "Don't you know *yet* how long ago it started?"

I put my glass down on Harry's desk. It was cold and steadying against the hot sweat of my palms. I hated to let it go.

"Dolly and I went to kindergarten together," Joe said. His statement had dignity and depth; to him, what he had said was the most important thing of all: that he had known her so much longer than I, if not half so well.

All right, I thought; now you listen to me.

"Sure, you knew her for years and years before I showed up. She used to tell me how many times you asked her to marry you and how many times she turned you down. And how you wouldn't give up. How even when she married me you wouldn't admit you were through, you wouldn't admit that maybe it was possible she could prefer someone else to the great Joe Spencer, country gentleman—dead broke."

He stood up, his fists clenching.

"You're asking for it, Frank."

Harry jumped up too.

"You two just wait a minute, will you?"

But Harry couldn't stop it. Nobody could. Because I had not only taken Joe's girl, I had taken part of his pride, too, and all of some bright ideal he had made from that girl and that pride. And in the long run, I thought, what I had tarnished for him he had had to destroy. That was what had brought us to this inevitable point.

"You're both acting like kids," Harry said. "Why do you have to argue now?"

That was a good question, and what it meant was: Dolly's dead, so what's the good of all this?

"I'll tell you what we've got to argue over," I said. "Dolly didn't commit suicide. Somebody else drove that Jaguar into that rock."

Joe sat down abruptly, his mouth falling open a little, his eyes opening wide.

Harry's voice was hot with anger. "I've tried to be decent to you, Frank, you'll have to admit that, but you're taking this idiotic thing too far. I told you there was no question about how Dolly died."

"Somebody who was alone with her," I said.

Joe's lips twisted. "Why, you dirty—"

"Has anybody seen my glasses?" George said. None of us had heard him come in, but now I heard him take a couple of heavy steps into the room. "Can't see a goddamn thing without 'em."

Walter took his pipe out of his mouth and laughed. The sound was loud and relieved.

"I don't see anything funny. I'm practically blind. Did I leave 'em in here, Harry?"

I turned and went around the edge of the desk toward the window where Walter stood. Muscles trembled in my legs and the armpits of my shirt were soggy with sweat.

"Good God," Harry said. "Have a drink, George. Come on in."

"I don't want a drink, Harry, I only want my glasses."

"Well, have one anyway."

George shook his head. He was blinking even in the dim light of Harry's desk lamp. "I got to find my glasses. I guess I must have left 'em out at the pool. I'll send P.B. out." A small frown pulled his brows together. "Say, I didn't interrupt anything, did I?"

"Not a thing," Joe said.

George nodded. He had spent a whole lifetime coming into rooms just after something had happened or going out of them just before something happened. He was in the Navy during World War II and they made him supply officer on an old bucket of bolts on the Australia run. George told me later that the only time the old tub heard a shot fired in anger during three solid years of war was in 1945 when a kamikaze came out of nowhere and went in fifty yards off the bow—and George was in the head at the time and missed the whole show.

There was a quick tap of high heels in the hall. Maggie and Ellen swept into the room.

"Pee-yew," Maggie said. "How do you characters stand those cigars?"

"Have yall seen my glasses?" George said.

"They're on the hall table," Ellen said.

Walter's hand closed on my arm.

"Let's go get those pills I promised you, Frank, before we forget."

His pressure on my arm was subtle but powerful. We moved across the room. I could feel Ellen's eyes on me curiously; her stare made my hands and feet feel too big.

"This room is enough to give anybody a headache," Walter said.

We went out into the wide hall and Walter closed the door behind us.

"Now you've done it," he said. "You and your big mouth."

There was a grandfather clock on the landing of the great stairway. Like the dining table and a marble-top table in the living room and the huge bed in Harry's room, it was from the old house, the one that had burned in 1864. Harry had moved the clock to the landing after he had come home from the Pacific, when he had taken down the portrait of Dolly's mother, which had formerly hung there, and stored it in the basement. Harry had never had any use for Dolly's mother. She wasn't a Thompson at all, he would say, even in Dolly's presence; she was too sickly and too mousy and too much of a furniture duster. I had the secret feeling that Dolly agreed with him and it made me ashamed for her.

Walter held my arm while we went up the stairs past the clock to the second-floor hallway. I didn't resist. I seemed to have been on my feet forty days. They were like great weights I had to lift up each step.

"You in your old room?"

I nodded. We went down the hall and into the huge corner bedroom Dolly and I had always had when we spent a night or a week end at Old Hundred, which had been quite often.

"You keep your goddamn pills to yourself," I said.

He shut the door. I was surprised at the hard bright interest in his usually bland eyes.

"What was it you were going to say down there, Frank?"

I sat down on the huge feather bed. "Nothing important."

"You were about to make an accusation."

"I told you, Walter. It was nothing important." I know you people, I thought. I know the way you stick together.

He smiled suddenly and his face became as disarming as usual. It was easy to get mad at Walter but you couldn't stay mad at him; he wouldn't let you. He made you feel you were being too childish.

"Walter," I said, "I . . . I guess I'm a little jumpy."

"Don't blame you."

He sat in an easy chair beyond the bed, crossed his legs comfortably, and took a pipe out of his pocket. He looked easily informal; yet he had deliberately rushed me out of Harry's study before I could say whatever I had been going to. He badly wanted to know what that was, and I remember the terror I had seen in his wife's face when I had told her someone had killed Dolly.

"Walter," I said, "what are you and Maggie afraid of?"

His smile wavered briefly but his eyes began to go over my face less penetratingly. I had said too much again, had disclosed how little I knew about anything.

"Afraid of? Death and discomfort. And ridicule, I suppose."

It was all getting to be a little too much for me. I wanted to lie back in the comforting lap of the huge bed and let its soft mattress swallow me. It was a little too much for me that for some reason Maggie and Walter Lee were afraid of what I might learn about Dolly's death.

"You were always a guy," Walter said, "with a positive talent for jumping to wrong conclusions."

His eyes were going over my face carefully again; they missed nothing, but now his stare had become professional.

"You know, Frank…" He put his round head over to one side and smiled the famous disarming bedside Lee smile that had come down to him through generations of Lee doctors. "You want to take it easy for a while."

One part of me was irritated; another part slipped with treacherous ease into the old comforting sense of being looked after by Walter Lee, a feeling shared by most of Huntsville. There had been a physician named Lee in the town in its first decade and there had been one ever since. At present, the town was divided in its opinions as to whether Walter could ever fill the shoes of his father, old Dr. T. A. Lee, since he had been trying only ten years. But the odds were beginning to shift in his favor.

At any rate, Huntsville placed the sort of implicit confidence in all doctors named Lee that only undertakers and Baptist ministers usually have to endure, and not so very many of them. It was grotesque to find him disturbed because of what I might know about Dolly's death.

"You look worn out, Frank. I really will give you a sedative if you want me to."

I let my elbows go out from under me and lay back flat on the feather mattress. Almost immediately, I could smell Dolly. I could feel the warmth of her body, the long softness of it, taste the cool sweet cherry flavor of her lips; she was all around me in that mattress. I sank into my memories of her, and for one moment longer than all that had gone before, I didn't think I could bear it, could stand being without Dolly forever. A great mellow aching grief rolled up in me, majestic as the symphonies she had loved so much, and I longed for anything Walter could give me that would blot out everything.

Walter stood up and his movement broke the spell. Grief went out of me swiftly and effortlessly and I remembered that somebody had killed her and that I had sworn to her ghost that I would prove it.

"Listen," I said. "Don't believe I'm still crazy, Walter. Don't let any of them believe it, either."

"You never were. The Navy sent me all the facts on your case. Did they ever decide what caused your trouble?"

"You know everything else, you ought to know that too."

"Dolly?"

"Get the hell out, Walter."

"Hang loose, Frank," he said. "Isn't that what they say in the Navy?"

"That's what they say."

"And let sleeping dogs lie. That's what we say here."

The door closed behind him. I wriggled hard down into the mattress and tried to find Dolly again. Then I rolled over and looked up at the starched underside of the canopy over the bed. Dolly had said she was going to have that canopy taken down and cut up into dish towels, but she had never got around to it. I remembered the exact inflection of her voice, the way her lips had pursed and moved, when she had first said that about the dish towels. I remembered the exact shape of the small hollow where her neck and shoulder met, the exact golden shade of the fine faint downy hairs that grew on her body, the exact pitch of her restrained little murmurs in my ear. I remembered everything and in the memory gave myself again to that mellow aching grief surging up like the sounds of symphonies.

Three weeks after Dolly and I were married, there was a dance at the Country Club. I did not want to go, but Dolly said we had to; if we didn't go to this first one, she said, we would never be able to get up the nerve to go to any of the others.

It was crowded and hot and uncomfortable at the Club and everybody was drunk but Dolly, who had decided it was a good time for her to keep clearheaded. I had intended the same thing, but as the evening wore on, I visited the bar more and more often. There I could huddle on a stool out of the way; there I could be by myself; there I did not need to stand miserable and alone on the dance floor and watch other men dancing with Dolly. There I could pretend not to hear them whispering.

Maggie Lee came in and perched on a stool beside me.

"Hello, Frank," she said. It startled me and I spilled my drink. In nearly three hours, only three other people—Harry Thompson, Dolly, and the bartender—had spoken directly to me.

"Hi." I put my glass down. My hand was shaky and I was beginning to have a little trouble focusing my eyes.

"What are you going to do about it?"

The bartender, without being told, put a bourbon and ginger ale in front of her. He had been at the Club a long time. We had lived at the same boardinghouse before I married Dolly.

"Do?" I said. "About what?"

"The way they're treating you."

I picked up my glass and drained it.

"Let 'em eat cake," I said.

"You're tight, aren't you?"

"So's everybody. Tighter'n hell. Aren't you?"

"It's different with them."

"Goddamn right," I said.

"They don't have to prove anything."

"Go 'way, huh? Go 'way an' leave Frank alone, what say?"

"Listen, I want to help. Dolly is a love and I think you're going to be all right and I want to help you."

She was wearing a low-cut gown—she always wore low-cut gowns—and her breasts, tanned like the rest of her, loomed up out of it like great strained overage melons. She took her sun baths all over, she liked to tell everybody.

Kenny Parr came into the bar and saw her and stumbled over to us. Kenny Parr was always tight but tonight he was worse than usual.

"H'lo, Mag, ol' girl. Les have us a drink, huh?" He put his arm around her and looked down between her breasts. "Jeez Christ," he said.

"You've had enough to drink, Kenny."

He laughed vacantly and looked away from her neckline to me. He blinked and looked back at Maggie and pawed at her arm.

"You drinkin' with *him?*"

"You're disgusting," Maggie said.

He laughed again and took his arm from around her shoulders.

"I may be disgus—disgussin' but I'm disgussin' on my own money, huh, Mag? Not my wife's."

I looked up dully from the bar, knowing that I was going to have to get up and hit him, drunk as we both were. I was just in time to see a flash of white and then there was a loud pop and Kenny Parr reeled back against the bar, holding his cheek where

Dolly had slapped him as hard as she could. I had not even seen her come in.

I stood up and she put both her hands on my arm and looked over her shoulder at Kenny. There were tears running in small glistening streaks from her wide shocked eyes.

"Come on, Frank," she said. "Quick, before I kill him."

"I'll kill him for you," I said. I was suddenly cold sober. I looked at Kenny Parr's vacant faded sodden face with the red spot growing on its cheek and I actually did want to kill him.

"Good for you, Dolly," Maggie said.

"Please ... let's go, Frank."

She would not even let me wait to get her wrap. We went straight across the dance floor and out into the black summer night. It was hot outside, too, and I wished I had a convertible.

Dolly drove my battered old sedan, since she had not been drinking. She was an erratic driver and when she turned out of the gates of the Club she was still in second gear. The tires screamed madly. I looked back at the gracious white building with the long windows looking out on the golf course.

"So much for the Country Club," I said.

"No! I won't *let* them treat you like that, Frank, I won't!"

"Maybe I deserve it."

The tires screamed again and she braked the car to a halt in the middle of the road. She threw herself against me and I put my arm around her and held her tightly.

"Don't you *ever* say that again, Frank Sinclair, not *ever!*"

I put my hand on the smooth golden hair.

"All right. Anything you want, honey."

"You're alive, Frank, you're vital, you're rugged, don't you see? That's what they can't forgive, because they're old and worn out and only want to be left alone."

She held her head back from me and in the faint glow of the dash I could see tears streaking her face. Her small body pushed hard against me with her deep breathing and I felt the incredible glow of love all through me.

"Dolly," I said. I kissed her for a long time, moving my lips on hers. "Dolly, I love you so damn much."

She put her forehead against my shoulder.

"Frank... what if I'm worn out, too?"

"Don't talk like that."

"But I'm like them. They're no different from ..."

I kissed her to stop the words.

"You aren't like anybody, Dolly."

"It scares me sometimes, though. There's so much against us."

"What?" I said, feeling brave and protective. "What that we can't lick?"

She never did answer because another car blew loudly behind us and I had to let her go so she could drive on.

"Frank?"

"Yes."

"Let's go away. Let's leave Huntsville."

"I'll be damned if I will," I said. "Let a tinhorn like Kenny Parr run me out of town? Or Joe Spencer? Not me!"

"No," she said. "I suppose not."

I slid across the seat and put my hand on her leg.

"Ah, listen, honey. They'll come around. If they see what we have is ... real and good and true, they'll come around. And what do we care, anyway? We've got each other."

She took my hand from her leg and kissed it.

"That's right," she said. "As long as we have each other it'll be all right."

CHAPTER FIVE

I F I COULD HAVE GONE to sleep after Walter left, I wouldn't even
have bothered to get up and take off my clothes. But I lay there
a long time—tired, a little bewildered, feeling faintly unreal—
and sleep failed to come.

I got up and took off my shirt and tie. I wore no undershirt.
When I emptied my trousers pockets, in addition to the usual
change and odds and ends, I found the long smooth stone I had
picked up at the boulder that afternoon. I looked at it again, no
longer curious, wondering why I had even bothered to pick it up.
I was looking around for a wastebasket in which to drop it when
there was a light tap at the door.

I put the stone on the dresser and went to the door, forgetting
my bare chest. Ellen was standing in the hall.

"Do you have everything you need, Frank?"

I stared at her stupidly.

"I wanted to make sure you were comfortable."

"You did?"

She took a step or two into the room. She was wearing a
sedate robe over quite ordinary-looking pajamas. There was no
make-up on her face and she was obviously ready for bed; yet,
as always, she gave the impression of having just come from the
beauty salon. Her dark hair was immaculate and, in the light
from the one lamp on the dresser, her skin had a rich glow, as if
she might actually have bathed it in cream.

"I didn't think you'd care whether I was comfortable or not."

There was amusement in her eyes. She went farther into the room and I turned to follow her. My elbow struck the door and it swung almost all the way shut. I went to the closet and found a robe—one of Harry's—and put it on.

"I know," Ellen said. "We got off on the wrong foot. We always do, it seems. I don't know why."

"Maybe we were born that way. Maybe it's glandular."

She picked at the loose knot of the belt holding her robe around her.

"I'd hate to think that."

She swung away from me, the skirt of the robe flicking out gracefully.

"This was yours and Dolly's room." She wandered a little, looking at the big old bed, at the ladder-back chair in one corner and the high dresser, as if she had never been in that particular room before.

"I'm sorry about Dolly, Frank. I truly am."

"You could have been nicer to her when she was alive instead of sorry now."

She was in front of the dresser with her back to me, and for a long moment she stood still, rigid, looking down at it. I could feel her chill-steel power again, that atmosphere of bloodless but irresistible dominance that could reduce me to a stumbling hulk. The backs of my knees began to tremble and my palms became greasy with sweat. Then she turned, smiling at me, and the chill was all gone from her.

"None of us were as nice as we should have been. But let's be friends now."

She came toward me, still smiling. Her hands toyed with the knotted belt again. Now they pulled it tight, nipping the robe in around her small waist and outlining her body.

"After all," she said, "there's no reason we shouldn't be … friends."

She was so close I could look down into the fine-boned face and the rich dark eyes. A faint perfume rose almost imperceptibly from her lovely hair. Her lips glistened.

"No reason," I said.

It was ridiculous. I knew that. It would have been against everything Ellen Thompson believed and worshiped to have seduced me or anybody else. It would have been a denial of all her gods, a renunciation of her faith, which set above all things family and propriety and elegance and wealth, in that order, none of which would have been served by betraying Harry. Yet ...

"Try," she said. "Try to like me."

My hands were trembling. I looked down into that beautiful white face and felt the manhood running out of me, felt the purpose going with it, leaving nothing but futility. She had always been able to do that to me; I had never been able really to cope with her. She left me always either intimidated or quivering in murderous rage.

"I've always tried to ... like you," I said.

She turned and walked toward the bed. There was something precise and efficient about that walk, about the way she moved. She would make love that way, too, I thought—expertly, no doubt, with no waste motion, no fumbling haste, but with no permanence, either, like a highly trained pianist executing skillfully the work of a composer she does not understand.

She stopped by the bed, looking down at it.

"I always thought of you as a blind man," Ellen said. "It seemed as though you never could see anything." Her fingers touched the bed.

My mouth went hot and dry; while her fingers lingered there on the bed, I knew I wanted her. I wanted that hard efficient body. Was it the first time? Or was that the power she had held over me all those years? Was that what had made me a stumbling bumpkin in her presence?

Without knowing it, I had moved close behind her. She heard me and started to turn. I picked her up from behind and tossed her down on the bed as if she had been a fresh pillow.

"Frank!"

She said that one, startled word; then, for just a moment, she lay there unmoving, helpless, staring up at me with something in her face I had never seen there before. While I watched it, I was having her in my mind. I couldn't help it. I watched her and I had her, starting from the first, going through all of it, having her on the deep soft feather bed that had been mine and Dolly's. It lasted a long time, the way Ellen would know how to make it last, and it was just as I had known it would be, hard and efficient and with no waste motion, no lost time, no incomplete action; it was just the way I had imagined it and it could not possibly have been more different from the hot deep sweet wild eruption of having someone you love … and just before it reached its snakelike expert end, I put my hand against my face and clawed at my cheek, hard, my nails raking my flesh like talons. The swift stab of pain went beneath the roots of desire, cutting them, so that it was over as suddenly as it had begun; and at the same time, Ellen rolled over and stood up on the other side of the bed.

"You're crazy," she said. "Stark raving mad."

It was all clear now, all plain. She had known all along what gave her her hold on me; and when she had seen that day that perhaps it was not as strong at it once had been, that perhaps I was beginning to come out from under her spell, she had known just what to do. She would not have thought she would have to pay the price; she would not have thought she would have to pay more than, at most, a wet glance or two and a hand on my cheek and perhaps a bloodless kiss.

A faint beginning sneer distorted her fine mouth, but she was still immaculate; not a hair was out of place and she was no more flushed, no more discomposed than if she had been in church. That should have reduced me to impotence, should have made my hands clammy, my throat tight. It didn't.

"You asked for it," I said. "If you didn't want it, get out."

She moved swiftly around the bed toward the door. The sneer curved fully across her mouth.

"Cheap," she said. "I didn't really know how cheap and vulgar you are."

I no longer cared what she said to me. Somehow, in that moment when she had lain defenseless on the bed and I had stood over her, staring down at that strange something in her face that I knew now had been terror—in the shame of that moment I had found freedom from her.

"Vulgar is as vulgar does," I said. "Beat it."

But she was gone before I had finished, not even competing for the last word. Her footsteps went rapidly down the hall. A door closed.

I had a private bath. I stripped and went in and took a shower. It eased my muscles but it didn't do a thing for my mind. When I came back I got pajamas out of my suitcase. It was cool and dark and quiet in the room. I could smell the lingering scent of the perfume Ellen had used. I went over and lay on the deep feather bed.

I had never had any luck with women, I thought. The Ellen business was another example. First there had been Dolly, and now ...

Dolly.

But that wasn't the same, I thought. With Dolly, the bad luck had all been part of her not knowing what she wanted. With Dolly ...

But I couldn't dodge it. I couldn't dodge the fact that I had never had her, either. Not really, not completely, not in all the whispering nights. I had loved her but I had never had her.

Everything went well for Dolly and me before Leander.

Soon after we were married, I received a promotion from the power company so that my work was all in the office and all done by four-thirty. Before Dolly, I would have hated such confinement. But as it was, I welcomed the change and rushed happily home each day.

The day Leander came, I found her lying across the bed, bundled in a huge loose robe—one of mine—and not quite sound asleep, so that she was a round warm bundle with a child's face smiling dreamily up at me, her short hair golden against the white of her fragile skin.

I leaned down and kissed her cheek. She rolled drowsily over and opened her eyes wider, still smiling. The robe had fallen open. She had nothing on under it, but Leander was clutched between her small breasts.

"What the hell is *that?*" I said.

She lifted the Teddy bear and looked at it.

"Harry brought it."

"Has he been here?"

"He stopped by right after lunch."

"Well, what did he leave that overstuffed mouse for?"

Dolly frowned. She pulled the Teddy bear back down to her breast. It looked absurd against her glowing white skin.

"It's company for me," she said. "Its name is Leander. I think it's a nice gift."

It was just like Harry, I thought, to bring such a damn-fool present to a grown woman. I watched her hug the ridiculous thing again. Almost immediately I hated it. I was even jealous of it. It seemed to me a live thing, lying between her breasts, where I alone belonged.

"This has got to go, Dolly."

I plucked the Teddy bear out of her arms and tossed it across the room and sat down on the bed.

She sat up swiftly. I slipped my arms around her, under the robe. She was warm, soft. I bent my head to her flesh, but before

I could touch it she twisted out of my arms and stood up. She looked wildly around, saw Leander supine against the wall, and rushed to pick him up.

"You didn't have any right to do that, Frank Sinclair! Leander's mine!"

"For Christ's sake," I said. "You can have him, then."

Her lovely lips pouted above the Teddy bear's stupid face.

"He's only a Teddy bear," she said. "Don't be mean to him."

"The hell with it. I don't care about it one way or another."

She took a bow tie of mine that lay across the back of a chair. "I'll put your tie on it, Frank. That'll make it all right, won't it?"

I watched her knot the gaudy tie around Leander's neck. Things were going around irritably in my head. Long periods of silence, cryptic remarks, nights when I had awakened to find her moving restlessly around the apartment. Down inside of me, the first faint beginnings of fear moved sickeningly.

"Dolly?" I said. "Do you love me, honey?"

She smiled at me over Leander's beady-eyed face.

"What do you think?"

"I think I'm scared."

"Of me?"

"For us."

She came toward me swiftly, carrying Leander in the crook of her arm. The robe was not buttoned at all. She swept the other arm around my head and pulled it close against her bare stomach. I could feel her fingers move in my hair, but for the first time since we had married, I did not want her physically. I knew I could have her, I knew that was what she was offering. But not a minute ago, all she had wanted was the gift Harry had brought, the toy that meant ... what?

"I love you, Frank. Don't worry about that. Only ..."

I closed my eyes tightly. The fear blew up like a great balloon in my belly.

"Only what?"

"Only...don't be so...don't *think* about...differences so much."

I twisted my head and opened my eyes. I could see past her hip and through the bedroom door to our living room. The apartment was a shambles because it was not Easter's day to come. Dolly, personally, was the cleanest person I ever knew; nothing delighted her so much as hot water and scented soap and big soft towels. I never knew her to go through a day without at least two baths, often three or more. But she had no more conception of the use of the broom or the clothes hanger or the wastebasket than a two-year-old. For a week or two we had groped our way among the hordes of little shoes, great clouds of discarded lingerie and dresses and skirts and filmy stockings, discarded letters and half-finished books and open boxes of chocolates and broken jewelry and untidy stacks of phonograph records. Then one day Easter had appeared. Easter had served Dolly since childhood, but we had both bravely resolved to do without her, since I obviously could not afford her, and since we were not—at first—going to use any of Dolly's money, a substantial sum left independently to her by her father.

"I couldn't stand it any more," Dolly had said. "I can't stand a mess. Not even my own."

I had refrained from mentioning that she could have cleaned it up herself.

"All right," I said, "but this is the only thing you're going to pay for."

"I can't help thinking about differences," I said now. "You would too if you were in my place."

"I know. But try anyway. You're so fine when you're yourself."

She pulled my head around so that my lips were against her skin. Suddenly I was angry. It's always on her terms, I thought indignantly. When I wanted her she pushed me away.

"And try to like Leander. I just like him because he's company and because Harry brought him."

She stroked my cheek. Her stomach was warm and soft against my lips. In the anger she had aroused, there was desire, too; I thought bitterly that God was unfair to let men reduce themselves to such utter helplessness over women.

"If you want me to, I will."

I put my arms around her again and this time she didn't push me away. But it wasn't total. As always, there was some last secret we never learned together. And when it was all over, I saw she still clutched Leander in one thin determined hand.

That had been years ago, but to me it was as real as if it had happened an hour before. Eventually, I slept; not soundly, not restfully, but in the sort of nightmarish stupor from which you awake more exhausted than ever. In my dreams, I floundered in the soft oozing sand of a limitless beach. A dish towel floated down from the canopy over me. It grew monstrous as it neared my face. Just before it fell on me, the great sucking lips of the sand closed over my head and I woke up.

I was greasy with perspiration. Everything was pitch-black. I was panting loudly, like an old hound on an August day. Right away, darkness and panting and all, I knew someone else was in the room.

I tried to stop panting. Over to my right something was darker than the darkness. It moved ever so slightly, stopped, moved again. Then it was gone. I heard the tiny click of the latch on the heavy old door.

I was not sleeping under covers and I wore only pajama trousers. I rolled carefully off the bed, touching my toes gingerly to the soft rug, still half asleep and half fearful that I might touch the awful ooze of my nightmare. I groped toward the door. My foot struck the leg of a chair. I swore but the pain waked me fully. I found Harry's robe across the back of a chair, slipped it over my shoulders, and went to the door.

I opened it carefully. A lamp burned at the end of the hall, where the stair well began. It sent a sick light past the rows of blank doors. The whole house seemed asleep. But someone had been in my room. The darker patch had moved too definitely. The click of the latch had been too recognizable. And it had been no mistake, either, or why had the intruder made such a stealthy retreat?

A board creaked in the downstairs hall.

I ran lightly along the carpeting to the head of the stairs, grabbed the lamp, and held it out in front of me. Nothing moved in the dim shadows below. There was no sound. But someone was there. I could feel a presence, just as I had felt it in my room.

I hurried halfway down the stairs, leaned out with the lamp again. In the yellow circle it dropped into the darkness, I saw the edge of the huge front door swing slowly shut.

I put the lamp down, at the limit of its cord, and ran down the stairs. I was not afraid. I could feel a strange fever in my chest, an odd shortness of breath. The intruder had made a mistake. In the time it had taken me to get out of bed and into the hall, he could have regained his own room and been free to strike another time. But now he was cut off. Now he had to flee into the grounds. If I couldn't catch him there, all I had to do was to return to the house and find out who was missing.

It did not occur to me that the intruder might have been someone from *outside* the house.

On the broad porch of Old Hundred, I stopped and stared hard into the night. The moon had risen long before, but a thick cloud was between it and earth. There was little or no light. A chilly wind zipped around the corner, an early-morning wind. Dawn was not long away, from the feel of it.

I tried to spot darkness moving against the skyline. There was no sound anywhere except that of the wind and of leaves rustling in the big oak trees. I moved to the porch rail, which was damp with dew.

Something scraped, no louder than a match striking, far down the porch. I raced toward the sound. Again, something darker than the darkness moved, and I made out the plain out-line of someone running away from the house.

My feet burned and stung on the porch floor. Then the grass of the lawn was cool and damp under them. I couldn't see a thing except, far ahead, that moving darker darkness, but I remembered that the lawn was clear of shrubbery on that side of the house. I ran as hard as I could into the inkiness in front of me.

A thin hot grip closed across the top of my foot. I cried out and plunged headfirst, the entire momentum of my body carry-ing me forward and down. I struck the ground full length, barely getting my hands and arms in front of me. My breath went out of me. I lay still, almost stunned.

I could hear running footsteps now that my own were qui-eted. The intruder was getting away. I groped in front of me, try-ing to find something solid to grip, with which to pull myself to my feet. My hand closed on something thin and strong and I pulled at it. It resisted and then came up out of the ground like a thinly rooted plant; it was a croquet wicket.

I got painfully to my feet and went forward carefully, nudg-ing my feet ahead, feeling for more croquet wickets. When I knew I had passed the playing grounds, I ran ahead. There were shrubs to my left now, and then they ended and I swung to the left and felt under my feet the cold flagstones of the terrace around the swimming pool.

I stopped, looking carefully ahead. Nothing moved. I stood there a full minute, letting my eyes get well used to the dark-ness. The bushes that lent privacy to the pool provided plenty of cover for the intruder, if he was still there. I stood carefully facing them. For the first time, it occurred to me that whoever I was chasing might be dangerous.

But I was too excited to be afraid. I *knew* now—no one would be able to doubt it any more—that I had been right. Someone was afraid of what I would find out about Dolly. All of them knew by now that I did not believe in the "suicide," and one of them had seen the necessity for action.

Gradually I made out the diving tower, angular against the night sky, and the six-foot apron of tile that edged the pool on all sides. From the dark smooth surface of the water itself I caught stray glints when the moon broke thinly through the clouds. Beyond the pool was a low-roofed bathhouse no one ever used. Plenty of hiding places there, in the shower rooms. I wished I had a flashlight. There could be no greater pleasure than to back that elusive patch of darkness against the bathhouse wall and shine a flashlight beam full into its face. Then we would see. Then we would settle matters. No matter when they had started.

I started forward across the flags toward the tile apron. The chilly wind blew across the pool, bringing little faint flecks of moisture with it. The tile was cold and clammy under my feet. It was expensive and beautiful but dangerous, I had always thought. Too slippery. Water made it worse. But then, I had always been afraid of pools, tile or no tile....

The footsteps were right behind me before I heard them. I whirled, got halfway around. Someone crashed into my back and side. Hands shoved at me and my feet went out from under me. I saw the spindly rise of the diving platform against the sky. It was going in a curious half circle about my head, and then the water of the pool was cold all around me and darker than anything I had ever experienced.

He thinks I still can't swim. My thoughts thrashed madly while I sank in the dark glistening shocking water. He doesn't know they made me learn. I kicked frantically and shrugged my arms out of Harry's robe. The intruder would be waiting up there on the tile. He would be waiting for me to drown, but it wouldn't take him long to see that I wasn't going to do that, that he would have to do something else. And he could take his time while I kicked and paddled in the middle of the pool. He could take all the rest of the ...

My head came up into the black terrifying air and I opened my mouth and gulped a great searing chestful of it and went back under again.

If only I could stay under. If only I could hold my breath till dawn came ... or if only I could call out. But we were too far from the house for anyone to hear me. Not with all of them asleep.

I had been a fool. I had let that elusive figure lead me straight to the pool, the one place where he must have thought my death could be made to look accidental. Drowned, the coroner would rule, while swimming alone at night. Well, I would not drown. But I couldn't stay underwater either. Already my head was beginning to swell and explode into tiny Roman candles.

No. I was going to have to come up. I was going to have to face him in the worst possible circumstances. And I was going to have to do it now, before the last Roman candle went off.

I kicked my feet and went up. When my head came out of the water, I flicked it backward, tossing my hair back, clearing the water from my eyes. I stayed as low as I could, keeping my mouth and neck underwater. The chlorinated water burned my nostrils as I drew in deep breaths of air. I could feel the chill of the water going through to the bone.

A dark figure was standing motionless under the diving tower. I could tell nothing about it, whether whoever it was was big or little, lean or fat.

That figure had meant to kill me. Anyone who had ever known me would have known I couldn't swim. I had taken a lot of ridicule because of it. But no one in Huntsville could have known that swimming had been one of the first things the Navy had forced me to learn in reorientation school. When that figure had come hurtling out of the darkness behind me, when it had thrown its weight—I had the impression, remembering, that it had not been a particularly big person—against me, it had meant that I should go into the pool, hard by the diving tower, where the water was deepest. It had meant that I should drown.

"You son-of-a-bitch," I said. "Come out where I can see you."

The figure did not move. I was treading water carefully, not wearing myself out.

"I learned to swim," I said. "I fooled you, goddamn you."

Still the figure did not move. Its stillness and my predicament made me suddenly, furiously angry.

"I'm coming," I said. "I'm coming after you again."

I struck out in my floundering crawl for the side of the pool. Almost immediately, the figure moved back from the tower, into the shadow of the bushes. But I could see it working rapidly around the pool toward where I was swimming. It was carrying some sort of club.

Whoever it was would be at the ladder—anywhere I chose to come out—before I could get there. And I would be helpless against anyone standing over me.

I whipped my body around in the water and stroked hard for the other side.

Over my shoulder I saw the shadow moving rapidly the other way around the pool. It was going to be a race. Fury lent power to my inexpert strokes and my body leaped through the water. But the dark figure was running hard, and before I was halfway there I knew it was no use. I pulled around again and headed for the diving tower. But that was no use either. Only anger kept me going. I thrashed in the middle of the pool like a harpooned whale. I cursed that flitting shadowy figure, wasting my precious strength with every word.

But I had no chance. I couldn't win that frenzied game of hide-and-seek. Every move I made foamed the water around me white as cotton, so that I was as easily followed as if I had had headlights. And I could not swim far enough underwater to do myself any good. The Navy had not thought to teach me that.

I don't know how long the absurd chase went on. It ended as it had begun, with me treading water in the middle of the pool and that evil shadowy figure almost lounging under the diving tower.

At least I was still alive. And if I could tread water until dawn, until someone else came to the pool, the only way he could get to me would be to dive in and swim to me. I couldn't think of anything I would rather he would do. I could almost feel his neck in my fingers.

"All right," I said. My breath was coming hard, burning my throat. I knew I ought to save it, but I couldn't. "All right. It's a standoff. Why don't you come and get me?"

If he would only say something. If he would only once come out of the deep shadows of the bushes or of the diving tower, so I might at least tell something about him ...

A sharp gust of the early-morning wind cut thinly across my neck and shoulders where they rode up out of the water. Perhaps it was the same gust that, at last, blew the cloud from in front of the moon. The darkness faded rapidly into a pale glow. The figure under the diving tower almost jumped toward the bushes. Something clattered on the tile. Then the moon made things as clear as in those dull minutes of preglow before the sun comes up; I had one final glimpse of the intruder, clearer now but still not clear enough for me to fix any details of it in my mind, scrambling into the shrubbery. But the one impression I was able to get was indelible. In that last glimpse, I saw something profoundly and terribly familiar. I could not identify what it was, but it told me for sure that the intruder had been someone I knew.

I swam to the nearest ladder, pulled myself out of the pool, and lay down. It was chilly on the wet tile in the predawn wind. But after a time I felt the tile begin to turn warm under me. Blood was moving in my body, keeping it alive, keeping it functioning.

I got up and went to the diving platform. Just beside it, still and deadly on the tile, there was a two-foot length of pipe, the same kind of which the diving tower was made. I picked it up and tossed it into the bushes, marking the spot. I thought I knew who had dropped that pipe there on the tile. But if my hunch proved wrong, perhaps there would be fingerprints on it.

I took off my wet pajama pants and rolled them in a tight ball. Then I walked across the lawn toward the house, buck naked. The first rays of dawn had topped the horizon, but I didn't care. I squeezed the water out of the pajama pants twice.

I put them back on when I reached the house. You could never tell who might be up, even at that hour.

CHAPTER SIX

HARRY AND ELLEN kept a decanter of brandy on the sideboard. In the tattletale-gray light of dawn, I moved through Old Hundred to the big double doors into the dining room. Brandy was exactly what I needed.

I was about to go in when I heard the clink of glass. I sank back against the wall by the doors. In a moment they opened and someone backed out.

It was Ann Harold. She held a glass in her hand. It was full of brandy.

"You're up early," I said.

She straightened and whirled, startled. She did not spill the brandy. Swiftly she moved the hand holding it behind her.

"Oh. Frank. It must have been you I heard."

I pushed away from the wall. She moved her head up and down, looking inquisitively at me in my wet clinging pajamas.

"When?" I said.

"A few minutes ago. Coming in the back door."

There was brandy on her breath. I wondered how long she had been in the dining room. She was wearing a thin hip-length jacket over pajamas.

"Not me." But I knew who it had been. "Didn't you see whoever it was?"

"No. I was in the dining room. I couldn't sleep."

It was not my night. But it was lucky for her she hadn't seen anyone. That might have put her on his list, too.

"Neither could I," I said. "I went for a swim."

"In your pajamas? How odd."

"I'm a sleepwalker, you see. I walked right in and swam the breast stroke fifteen hundred meters and then got out and came in here for some brandy."

"I didn't even know you could swim."

"I'll bet you didn't." I reached out and took hold of her arm and pulled the glass of brandy from behind her. "What do you need this stuff for, Ann?"

She jerked her hand away and a little of the brandy slopped over on her fingers. An angry flush spread across her face.

"I couldn't sleep. Now I'm going back up and see if this will help. They say it will."

"Oh, it will, all right. Just like the one you had in there. Or was it two?"

Her thin, unpainted lips tightened.

"Let me pass, please."

"I want to know," I said. "You don't have to pretend with me." I didn't know why, but it had become important to me that she should admit how much she drank. It was such an insidious thing to keep secret in her own private little world.

"I don't know what you're talking about."

"I'm talking about your drinking too much," I said. "I want to know why you do it."

Her face grew harsh. She stepped back from me and looked at the brandy in her hand. She threw back her head a little and drank the brandy, all of it, in one gulp. I had never seen a woman drink like that before. It reminded me of a snake I had seen being fed a white rat at the State Museum. Seeing her drink was the ugliest thing I had watched since that snake.

She looked at me with anger and terror and defiance.

"Do you think I know why?" she said. "Do you think I'd keep on doing it if I did?"

There was nothing to say to that. She looked at me a moment longer, until the anger and the defiance were gone and nothing was left in her eyes but terror. She held out the brandy glass.

"Here. Souvenir for you."

It was sticky and warm. She went past me toward the stairs. I didn't try to go after her. I went into the dining room and put the glass back on the sideboard. I didn't want brandy any more. I wanted to go to sleep. I wouldn't have to think if I were asleep.

I made no noise going upstairs. It wasn't that the person who had pushed me into the pool might be waiting for me. The night's excitement was over. He would want no more of me than I did of him, would hold back until some better time, some better plan could be arranged. But I didn't want to face anybody else while I was wearing nothing but wet pajama pants.

I found the lamp halfway down the stairs, where I had left it. I took it back to its table in the upper hallway and went on toward my room.

"Frank?"

Ann stood in the door to her room, dressed as she had been downstairs, except that her hair was more neatly combed. Her face was solemn, composed, dead white.

"You still up?" I took a step or two toward her, then remembered my bare chest, my wet pajamas pants. I looked down at myself, wishing helplessly for the robe I had left at the bottom of the swimming pool.

"I just wanted … You must think I'm pretty awful."

"Me?"

"I never said or did anything like that in front of anybody before."

"Look, you don't have to …"

"It was awful of me to do it, but I feel better. I never admitted to anybody before that there was … anything wrong. Not even to myself."

"Listen," I said. "You don't have to feel bad because of me. You never will get down to where I've been."

"I've been pretty low. One time I...If I just knew *why*. If there was only some *reason*."

This was no time or place to psychoanalyze her.

"You go back to bed. Stop worrying about yourself. That never helped anybody."

"But don't you see what you've made me—"

"You would have done it sooner or later anyway. You didn't need me."

"I want to thank you, anyway."

I couldn't think of anything but how foolish I felt in those wet pajamas.

"Sure," I said. "I have to go, Ann."

Amusement glinted faintly in her eyes.

"How *did* you get so sopping wet? Really?"

I don't know why I said it. I had already made up my mind to keep it to myself. Perhaps it was the shade of warmth I had detected in her eyes; perhaps it was just that I badly needed to talk to someone.

"Somebody tried to drown me."

Her eyes got wide and shocked and she moved back against the jamb of the door, her hands behind her.

"I'm not crazy," I said. "I know what I'm saying."

"*Drown* you!"

"You said yourself downstairs you didn't know I could swim. Nobody around here knows I can, because the Navy didn't teach me how until they called me back this time. But somebody pushed me into the deep end of the pool tonight."

"Not on purpose. You *can't* mean that."

"Somebody came to my room and woke me up and ran. I followed to the pool, got careless, and got pushed in. When whoever it was found I could swim, he stuck around waiting for me to come out so he could get another whack at me. He was waving a two-foot pipe."

"But who would *do* such a thing?"

"I never got a decent look. As soon as the moon came out, he took off."

One slender white hand crept stiffly around her neck, clung there. Her shoulders bent inward in a shudder.

"Frank, was it ... the one I ..."

I nodded. "The one you heard come in the back door."

"But why would anybody want to drown you?"

I laughed.

"Same person who killed Dolly," I said.

Her eyes closed tightly and the hand slid away from her throat and, as if it were a muscular convulsion over which she had no control, her body thrust itself away from the doorjamb and up against me. I felt her hands, cold and firm and dry, slide up my back to my bare shoulders. Her head was buried against my shoulder and I could look down on her neat blonde hair and feel the whole length of her shuddering gently against me.

"Horrible," she whispered. "It's too horrible, Frank. I can't think about it."

The breath of her words whispered hotly against my skin, and for a second I was stabbed to the heart with an unbearable familiarity. I closed my eyes and in my delusion this was Dolly in my arms, this was her small tender body trembling against me, this was her exquisite breath on my flesh. Everything went away from me then—the long agonized months of vegetable-like silence, the nightmare trip to Huntsville on the train, the rock and its weird inscription, the hours at Old Hundred, the hostile faces, the dark figure moving in my room, the obscene hide-and-seek at the pool; it all went away from me like cigarette smoke toward an open window, and I was back with Dolly. I was back with her long enough to know that this was the nearest thing to completion there had ever been for me.

I squeezed my arms around her and pulled her more tightly against me, feeling the shudder go out of her, seeing her golded head go rolling back the way it always had, seeing her white delicate face turning up to me, its long lovely lashes going languishingly down over its blue eyes, and its lips tasting forever of cherries....

Ann flung herself out of my arms and back against the door. Her face was stricken. Her long hands clenched on her thighs. She was bent slightly at the waist. A sort of repugnance glared at me from her fixed dilated eyes.

"Why do you always have to... Can't there ever be anything but *that* with you?"

Dolly, I thought. Oh, Christ, Dolly, come back to me. I can't stand it, I never could stand it without you.

"Sorry," I said. I was not thinking about Ann. She wasn't hurt. It was just a case of mistaken identity. She would have to get over it the same way I would.

I went down the hall toward my own door, as if I were walking under water. She was still leaning over, her knees a little bent together, as if she were cold. She was looking down at the floor. As I watched, a tremor ran the whole length of her body, like a ripple on the surface of a pond.

I went into my room and closed the door. It was on the side of the house away from the morning sun and it was still dark. I dropped the wet pajama pants to the floor and fell naked across the bed. My hair was still wet but I was too tired to get up and dry it.

You've got to stop this, I thought. You can't go on living over every moment with Dolly. You have to get together a new life some way.

That was easily said. But I had found nothing to replace what her going had taken from me. I had found nothing that meant half the joy and pain and sorrow and splendor that living with Dolly had been—even after it all began to go bad and come apart, even after I began to know what a terrible mistake we had made.

We had lived on the upstairs floor of one of the tall old houses on Sycamore Street. It had been haphazardly converted into an apartment by Mrs. Kelly Barnes, whose husband had run away with a practical nurse and created one of the biggest scandals in Huntsville history. Mrs. Barnes, a cadaverous party whose eye gleamed with perpetual indignation, charged too much, furnished too little, and interfered too often. But, Dolly said, it was a cool, roomy place, and where else was there to live in Huntsville except at Old Hundred or on Sycamore Street?

In November, five months after we had been married, the power company began a rigid economy drive in its branch offices, subjecting each of them to a monthly inspection tour from the head office. The week the Huntsville branch was inspected, I didn't get home a single night before eight o'clock, including the night before my birthday.

That night, when I entered Mrs. Barnes's downstairs hall, odorous from age and Belle, a house cat as cadaverous and outraged as its mistress, I could hear the music from our sitting room. It was dark outside and beginning to be cold, so that the street lights had a frosty look. I was learning to like Dolly's music and I was hungry and it would be warm in the apartment and Dolly was waiting; I took the stairs two at a time.

"Mr. Sinclair!"

I stopped midway up the stairs, irritation flaring all over me. The old witch, I thought. The dried-up hateful old witch. I looked over the dark polished banister into Mrs. Barnes's lean suspicious face.

"We are going to have to do something about that music, Mr. Sinclair."

"What would you suggest?" I said. It was not as if we hadn't been through all this before.

Mrs. Barnes's sharp nostrils quivered. Her eyes raged. Like the whole town of Huntsville, she had taken an attitude toward me—after recovering from the initial pure amazement caused by my marriage to Dolly—of pained and pessimistic curiosity. I was easily the best-known man in town. Small obnoxious children pointed me out on the street. Women whispered behind my back in the supermarket (in which Dolly resolutely refused to set foot). Men with whom I did business looked at me with faintly veiled contempt. Everybody believed implicitly that I had married Dolly for her money, that I had achieved this by some dastardly machination not yet brought to light, and that sooner or later I would abscond with the bank account and, probably, a girl from the five-and-dime store. Mrs. Barnes, having had some experience in that sort of thing, was among the most devout believers in this theory.

"That music's just simply too loud," she said, smacking her lips over the criticism. "You'll just have to tell her to turn it down."

"She likes it loud. It's not all *that* loud, anyway."

Renewed indignation puffed out her slatted chest like a pouter pigeon's. "Well, then," she said. "Well, then, there'll just have to be an adjustment in the rent next month."

She folded her arms and marched off to the rear of the house. Belle slunk after her, purring malignantly.

Might as well ask Dolly to dye her hair as turn the music down, I thought. Kind of nerve-racking sometimes. But I'll be damned if *that* old monument is going to dictate to her about it.

I hurried up the steps, anxious to collect Dolly and go out to dinner. We had planned a birthday celebration and were going to drive nearly twenty miles to another town, where there was an excellent restaurant that served a planked steak Dolly particularly liked. We never ate at home any more; after a month or so of ludicrous meals, I had taken her in hand and taught her the bare rudiments of cooking, but even so, her lunches and dinners had never improved much. And she was never able to get out of bed in time to fix breakfast. Eating out was the only solution.

I opened the door into the small vestibule that led into our sitting room. It was dark in there, except for the orange glow leaping silently on the far wall, reflecting the fireplace. The music boomed up suddenly, a live thing in the room. Sometimes it could be like a third presence, a being I could not help considering an interloper.

I hung up my topcoat and stepped into the sitting room. She had probably fallen asleep on the big sofa in front of the fireplace, as she often did, waiting for me. But I could see the crown of her little yellow head over its back. There was another beside it.

For an instant, an intense hysterical fear flashed through me. Then I saw that the second head was Harry's. Their backs were to me as they sat staring into the fire. There was something about those heads, silhouetted by the weak flicker from the old second-story grate, some closeness, some affinity between them, that told me finally what for a long time I had not let myself think: that Dolly was not happy. I had taken her from Old Hundred and put her down in a situation with which she could only occasionally cope, and then only by the sort of fury with which she had attacked Kenny Parr at the Club, a situation in which she had to depend on a man who, not understanding her or even half the time believing completely in her reality, was equally unable to cope with her moods or her sudden passions, let alone the weird frenzied gaiety with which she gallantly attempted to conceal both. No, I had not made her happy, and, seeing their heads so closely together, I realized it at last, realized what I had done to her.

"Dolly?" I said.

She jumped up and whirled around and knelt on both knees on the sofa, looking impishly at me over its back and her folded arms.

"Happy birthday, Frank. Come kiss me."

Harry had turned, too, grinning at me. "Many happy returns," he said. It made me feel better to have Harry wish me that. When he said something, you always felt he really meant it.

I went to her and put my hands on her shoulders and kissed her cheek.

"Hello, Harry," I said. "Nice of you to come by."

"Harry's going to take us to Old Hundred for dinner," Dolly said. "Isn't that sweet? Easter's baked a cake for your birthday and Harry says even Ellen said for us to come."

"Miracles never cease," I said.

Harry cleared his throat and stood up.

"Birthdays are fine times." He smiled at Dolly and put his hand on her head and tousled her hair a little. "We always made a lot over Dolly's, you know. We'll do the same for you if you'll let us."

Gratitude almost choked me; I could never say Harry hadn't tried to help us, hadn't done his best to bring me into his and Ellen's and Dolly's circle. And perhaps he was succeeding at last, perhaps things could be made all right for Dolly and me after all. It was good that I had finally admitted that she was not happy. It was a healthy sign. That brooding underlayer I had sensed in her had already become so predominant, had already taken her so far from me. She would sit for long hours cuddling Leander and listening to the gloomy symphonies she loved (Dolly hated contemporary music more passionately than she hated cats, with which she would not stay in the same room, particularly the repellent Belle; she would not stay in the same room with, say, "The Four Temperaments," either), staring unblinkingly at the unprepossessing ceiling. Or she would be so frantically gay she bordered on the slapstick, while all the time, beneath the wild laughter and the frenzied whirl of her little body about the room and the feverish glitter of her eyes, I sensed that bitter sadness, that muffled drumbeat of melancholy, so that I could not help seeing that the gaiety was as forced as the transparent enthusiasms she showed for the "housekeeping" she was always going to begin next week.

"That's a new suit." Dolly's voice grew excited; it always did at the mere mention of handsome clothes. "Frank, you darling, that's a new suit!"

"I guess so." I had changed into it at the office in order to surprise her for the birthday dinner we had planned. "Like it?"

"*Love* it." She flung herself around the sofa—Dolly never walked anywhere—and against me. "Mmmmm. Feels good. Frank, it's so *right* on you."

It was not right on me because it had cost about three times what I could afford. But I had known she would like it. I saw Harry looking at the cut of the coat. He seldom wore anything but shabby jackets and rather baggy trousers himself, but that didn't matter; just looking at him you could tell he had clothes for any occasion, that he knew how to wear them all, would appear as comfortably at home in morning coat or tennis flannels as in an old linen jacket.

"That's good-looking," he said. "You didn't get that around here, Frank."

"I had to go to Charlotte last month. I... ah, went to that place you told me about." I was acutely self-conscious. My suit seemed suddenly pretentious, conspicuous. If I could only relax, I thought. I wished I hadn't bought the suit.

Harry nodded gravely. Dolly thrust herself back from me, looking up with her bright blue eyes full of some secret joy.

"I'll bet you think I didn't get you anything."

"That doesn't matter," I said. "It isn't gifts that count." It sounded naïve, but I meant it. I was always sounding naïve, it seemed to me.

"Come on. I can't wait to show you." She tugged at my arm. Past her, I could see Leander lying on the sofa.

"But listen ... about dinner. We've got reservations over in Trenton, Harry." I had looked forward for a long time to this special night with Dolly. I didn't want it spoiled under the cold contemptuous eyes of Ellen Thompson, even if it did mean that perhaps at last she was beginning to unbend toward me.

"Oh, Frank, don't worry about that. Harry wants us to come to Old Hundred."

"Of course," Harry said, "I don't want to break up ..."

"Oh ... no, no. It was just that I called this fellow over in Trenton and ..."

"But he *knows* me," Dolly said. "He's known me all my life and he won't *expect* me to show up. Besides, Easter baked you a cake."

She wanted to go to Old Hundred. I could see that. Well, God knows, I couldn't blame her. I looked around at the cluttered living room, at the dying fire in the grate. There was a faint odor of Belle in the room.

"And we're all going to get drunk," Dolly said. "We're going to get Ellen drunk, even. Aren't we, Harry?"

He smiled a little. It always disconcerted him when she teased Ellen, but he tried to be a good sport. Harry would have done anything to be a good sport.

"I don't know about that," he said. "We can try."

"We ought to do *some*thing with the old sourpuss." Dolly was the only person in Huntsville who was ever irreverent about Ellen. "Frank, come on, your present's outside."

"Outside?" Suddenly I was feeling very good. It was my birthday and Dolly was happy because we were going to Old Hundred and she was going to try to get Ellen drunk again. She was always trying to get Ellen drunk and winding up a little tight herself. "What the hell is it, a cow?"

I couldn't have sold that line to Fred Allen but we all thought it was funny. We thought it was so funny we laughed all the way down the stairs. Dolly was laughing so hard she didn't even scream when she saw Belle scowling and hissing in the lower hall.

Outside, it had grown colder. Dolly had not put on a coat and she got between Harry and me and made us both put an arm around her. She shivered exaggeratedly.

"Where's this cow?" I pretended to peer closely at the lawn.

"Maybe it's a bull," Dolly said. "Maybe I'm trying to make you feel insignificant."

"What a thing to say," Harry observed mildly.

"Of course," she told him, in a conversational voice, "it would take one hell of a bull to make Frank look insignificant."

"Dolly, for Christ's sake," I said. But I was secretly pleased, because her teasing implied an intimacy between us that Harry couldn't share; it allied the two of us, rather than leaving me the outsider of the trio.

We went around the corner of the house, laughing. Then the laughing ballooned in my chest and throat and choked me. I stopped dead still. I could feel the chilly night air on the back of my neck. Through a hole in my shoe, which I had intended for a month to have fixed, the ground was clammy and cold.

Dolly took her arm from around Harry and swung herself around in front of me and held me tight with both arms. The top of her head just fitted under my chin.

"Do you like it, Frank? Do you?"

I moved my head from side to side, clearing my throat. I could not take my eyes off the big dark Cadillac. It caught little glittering patches of light from the bare bulb high over the street. There was something richly contemptuous in the way it stood so motionless, so passive, so undisturbed.

"Dolly," I said, "for God's sake."

"Say you like it, Frank. I wanted you to have it so badly."

Harry moved and at last I looked away from the car and at him. He struck a match and held it to a cigarette. He was not looking at me at all, but in his face I saw that he knew how I felt, that he understood something Dolly never would understand.

We had not been going to use any of her money; not, that is, until Easter began to work for us three times a week. But after that, there was the leather luggage Dolly just couldn't resist for me and the $150 movie camera that she said I could use to make sexy movies of her if I would promise not to show them to strangers and the new Stromberg-Carlson that she had had the furniture store order for her even before we were married and the fifty-dollar check to the Community Concert

Association and the set of golf clubs that, of course, I just *had* to have because Dolly had read with alarm in an advertisement that nowadays more business was done on the nineteenth hole than in the office. What difference did it make if I couldn't play golf? I could *learn*, couldn't I? It looked simple enough to Dolly. And, finally, there had been a horse. I had peremptorily returned that, although Harry had volunteered a home for it, and it had taken her two weeks to forgive me. It was such a lovely horse, she said. It matched her hair. And I would have loved it if I had ever taken the trouble to get to know it.

"Isn't it a *gorgeous* car? You'll look like Gregory Peck or somebody, Frank. I can't *wait* to see you driving it."

Well, I paid the rent and bought the food. I paid the Country Club dues, too, even though the power company had bought me the membership. And I bought my own clothes. But the barriers were gone and there was not even an honest pretense any more that we didn't use Dolly's money. For months she had spent it exactly when, where, and how she pleased.

"Don't you like it, Frank?"

"Sure I like it, honey, sure ... I like it. It's just that ..."

"Just that what?"

"Nothing. Thanks, Dolly. It was just what I needed."

She laughed a little.

"Joe got me a discount. He got a hundred and fifty dollars off for me."

"On a Cadillac. That helped a lot."

Harry took the cigarette out of his mouth. It made a red arc in the darkness.

"If Easter's cake doesn't get eaten soon, she'll leave and go North," he said.

We got our coats and piled into the Cadillac and went to Old Hundred. Driving a Cadillac will make you feel better about anything, and I cheered up some before we got there. But something had gone out of the evening and we all knew it. Only

Dolly didn't know what it was. She only knew things were taut and strained and she could never stand that, except when she herself was causing it. She flung herself into the evening with that mad determined gaiety I had come to dread. She wanted us all to laugh and she made us all laugh, even Ellen. She wanted us all to be happy, too, but she couldn't manage that, so she tried to get us all drunk instead. She could not manage that, either, and before midnight she was curled in a big armchair, not exactly passed out, but the victim of too much frenzy and too much whisky and too much of something else I had never been able to define. She looked small and defenseless and childlike in the huge chair; she looked very much as she must have looked twenty years before when she had played too hard and too long on the great lawns beneath the huge trees of Old Hundred. I went for her coat and mine and came back and stood looking down at her for a minute. If only she could always be so peaceful, I thought; if only she never had to wake up and find me and all I've meant to her.

"She drinks too much," Ellen said. "Does she get that from her mother, Harry?"

The cool collected precise voice pricked sharply at my nerves.

"She doesn't do anything of the sort. You don't have any cause to say that, Ellen."

She shrugged. As I had so often, I wanted to slap her, strangle her, beat some human reaction out of her.

"I've just seen her like this so often. Of course, it's none of my affair. I suppose it *is* from her mother, isn't it?"

Harry frowned.

"Dolly's mother didn't drink at all. She never did anything worth a damn but carry Father's pipes around for him. She didn't know how to do anything else."

"Would you ... ah, hold my coat?" I said. I handed it to him and picked Dolly up. One of her hands slid up my arm and around my neck and her yellow head nestled down against my shoulder.

I carried her out to the new Cadillac. She weighed almost nothing. I loved to carry her. It made her seem so completely mine.

I curled her securely in the front seat of the Cadillac and got in beside her. Harry leaned in the window, spreading my coat around her.

"Sorry, Harry. She gets so damned excited."

He looked up at me. His head and shoulders were inside the car. "It would make her happy if you'd keep the car," he said.

"I know it would."

"But I suppose you're going to send it back."

"I have to. If I had any guts I could take it, but I don't. I *have* to send it back, Harry."

"Sure." He nodded and looked at Dolly. She lay sleeping very quietly, her head almost under his. He touched her cheek with his lips. Something lurched in my soul. There had been so much in that kiss. There had been so much that was perfectly plain and so much I could only guess at. It made me the outsider again. It recalled how close Harry and Dolly had always been, how far away from all that a man named Frank Sinclair was always going to be. Somebody had told me, long before I even knew Dolly, that she would never find a husband just right for her because Harry was the only man who fitted that description and he was her half brother. What had been a joke then had the bitterly triumphant ring of prophecy now.

"Maybe I will keep the goddamn thing," I said. "After all, she got a hundred-and-fifty-dollar discount, didn't she?"

CHAPTER SEVEN

I DREAMED of dish towels. Again they were floating down from the canopy of the bed. They fell wetly and one by one into my face. Then one fell that was not wet. It flicked sharply against my cheek and snapped back, making a flat popping sound. The sound came again and again and the end of the dish towel kept snapping into my face. It didn't hurt, but it woke me up.

Outside, in the brilliant morning sun, firecrackers were popping. It was the Fourth of July.

It was hard to focus my eyes, to make my body wake with my brain. It was like getting out of a hot deep Japanese bath, with the blood turned to a thick sirup inside you.

I took a shower and dressed slowly. I had no suit except the gray hard-finish I had worn the day before. I did have an extra shirt or two and clean underwear. I put on the trousers to the suit and a white shirt, which I left open at the neck. I rolled the sleeves halfway up to my elbows and that was as close as I could get to sports clothes.

I took my watch off the dresser and put it on. I slipped my pocket change and the long smooth stone I had picked up at the rock into my pocket. In the mirror, as I combed my hair, I saw that my eyes were red-rimmed. The skin stretched across my nose and cheekbones was old and tired, faintly malarial. And the scar on my forehead, where I had been hit with a beer bottle in a brawl at the Officers' Club in Sasebo, Japan, lifted the inner edge of one eyebrow perhaps a quarter of an inch, giving me a questioning look. My Adam's apple stood out sharply under my chin and I realized how much weight I must have lost in the hospital; my neck was as thin and scrawny as that of a dressed turkey.

Let it go, I thought. What does it matter? You aren't signed to play Rhett Butler.

The house was quiet when I went downstairs. The ornate hands of the clock on the landing stood at eleven-fifteen. Outside, the sun beat down and reflected brilliantly from Harry's carefully trimmed grass. The popping of firecrackers had stopped. Almost instantly, the glare gave me a headache. I needed breakfast but the thought of food made my head ache worse. I walked slowly toward the pool. It was a hot day and sweat was running freely on my back and chest and forehead before I had got around the corner of the house.

Soon I could hear the high voices of women laughing and a deeper voice I recognized as Joe Spencer's. I quickened my step, passing the croquet grounds and the shrubbery. Then I came out into the open area around the pool. The diving tower rose gauntly beside it.

Ellen was on the high board. Her shoulders squared, her arms rose gracefully from her sides, and her body tensed. She reminded me of a jet aircraft trembling powerfully on the deck of a carrier. Her body, in its cold machined symmetry, was as cleanly beautiful as the jet, and both, in their arrogance, were unspeakably cruel. Then she was in the air, hurtling toward the water. It parted, closed around her again with scarcely a splash. She came up and tossed her head back, flinging glittering drops from her white cap.

"Terrific!" Joe's voice had a deep note that carried well out of doors, like the voices of his hounds; he could modulate it so that, indoors, it was intimate and warm, yet male beyond question. It was quite a successful voice with women. It made my teeth grind to hear it.

He stood by the pool with an arm around Maggie. She was wearing a strapless bathing suit and a light robe. Joe's arm was under the robe, pulling it back so her tanned legs showed. He was thin but dark hair covered his chest.

Ellen took three graceful strokes toward the ladder that rose beside the diving platform. Beyond Joe and Maggie, I could see Ann and Peggy sun-bathing in deck chairs. George was climbing up the diving platform. I couldn't see Walter or Harry.

"Now watch George," Joe was calling. "He's going to try a snap roll, I think."

"Let me out of the way, then." Ellen pulled herself up the ladder.

"Snap roll, my foot," George said. "I'm lucky if I don't break my neck every time I jump off this damn thing."

"You be careful, George," Peggy called. "George! Did you hear me?"

George went down like a two-by-four thrown from a window. He hit the water with a tremendous slapping splash. Joe roared with laughter. George came up, grinning foolishly.

"George!" Peggy called. "You stop that diving this minute, George Johnson!"

It was a gay party there around Harry's kidney-shaped swimming pool. Here was a group of well-to-do young people having themselves a holiday ball. It was going to be a shame to break it up.

I reached the diving platform as Joe took off in a perfect swan dive. He had always been excellent off the high board or at any other sport. I walked to the iron ladder to wait for him, looking for my robe at the bottom of the pool. It wasn't there.

Maggie dived from the tile and swam in a long violent crawl toward me. Joe came up, tossed his dark hair back from his eyes, and lay back and floated. Let him float, I thought; I can wait and he can't hide.

Maggie's outstretched fingers brushed against the top rung of the ladder. She pulled herself in to it and stood on the bottom rung, looking up at me. Without make-up, her face looked older. There were half-moon shadows under her eyes.

"Sleepy-head," she said. "Where are your trunks?"

"I don't have any," I said. "Do I need trunks to swim here?"

"Ellen wouldn't care for you in the raw."

"Ellen wouldn't care for me in a Brooks Brothers suit."

Maggie climbed up the ladder and stood beside me, dripping. She smelled of chlorine and wet cotton, and when she took off her bathing cap her dark hair fell past her wet tan shoulders. She still had very good legs and her stomach was not quite obtrusive in the tight swimming suit.

Joe pulled himself up out of the pool beside us. I had not seen him swimming to the ladder. He was lean and tanned and muscled.

"Morning," he said. His voice was not particularly hostile, but his eyes crinkled at the corners, as if he were bracing himself for an attack. He put his arm around Maggie again, his big hand falling familiarly along her hip.

"You want to talk to me here and now in public?" I said. "Or would you just as soon take a walk somewhere?"

"I'd as soon bust you in the snout. You're getting on my nerves, Frank."

He took his arm from around Maggie and brushed past me. His wet shoulder left a damp smear on the sleeve of my shirt and I turned to go after him. Maggie caught my wrist. I pulled loose, not gently, and followed Joe.

There was no one in the water now and it was flat and unruffled and so clear I could make out the label on a sun-tan-lotion bottle lying on the bottom. There should have been a robe there, too. Maybe there should even have been a body, undulant and bloated in the green silent depths.

Peggy Johnson took off her dark glasses and looked up at me from the deck chair beside Ann. Beyond them, I could see Joe stretched out on a blanket between George and Ellen.

"Hello, Peggy," I said. She muttered something and pulled her halter up, as if my proximity compromised her. Dolly had always suspected Peggy of wearing falsies, but she had the best legs in Huntsville. Even Dolly would admit that.

"Peggy," I said, "when are you going to stop kissing Ellen's fanny?"

She flounced out of the chair as if there were a roach in it.

"Well, I *never!*"

She strode off toward the house. She was wearing tight shorts and her little rump twisted indignantly as she walked. I was surprised how cute she looked; it was hard to think of Peggy as cute.

Ann stared up at me, open-mouthed, from her deck chair by the one Peggy had vacated.

"Lady," I said, "you ain't seen nothing yet."

I went past her to where George and Joe and Ellen lay sunning themselves. I looked down at them. Ellen had two little cotton patches over her eyes to shield them from the sun. She wore a brief two-piece bathing suit, but she did not look so exposed in it as Ann or Peggy or Maggie did in fuller garments.

George rolled over and blinked up at me. A crease ran down one side of his face, where his cheek had lain against a wrinkle in the blanket. His eyes, without his glasses, were weak and red.

"Let's you and me go get a beer," he said.

George Johnson was two people. One was the businessman who had inherited from his grubby father a small but highly profitable department store of the second-rate variety, who had spread this business into nine towns and built it into one of the biggest single retail enterprises in the state, and who was easily Huntsville's wealthiest man. That George was formidable.

But when you encountered the second George, and if you knew the first, you cursed Peggy Johnson and her grasping climbing nature for the bumbling clown she had made of him. I looked down at that George, the second one, looked at his hesitant smile, like that of a child making friends with a strange dog, and shook my head.

"You can't change anything," I said.

Then, for the first time since I had come back to Old Hundred, in the sudden shrewd intense blue of his eyes and in the way his hands became quite still, like two leashed hounds, lean and capable and ungentle, I saw the other George.

"It's your business, Frank."

"Tell your boy friend. Tell him about my business, George."

Joe was lying on his stomach. He stirred and turned his head the other way, ignoring me. Ellen had not moved at all.

"George," I said, "would you tell your buddy there to get up on his goddamn feet?"

Muscles rippled and tensed in Joe's back. My knees were beginning to shake and my mouth had gone dry.

Ellen took the patches off her eyes and looked up at me, shading her face with a blue-veined hand so delicate the sun almost shone through it.

"Is there something you want, Frank? Because I don't care for that kind of language at all."

"That's all right what you don't like," I said. "I got business with Jeb Stuart there, if he'll get up and attend to it."

Joe rolled over. His eyes were narrowed and his lips were pulled into a thin line. I wondered if he had looked that way the night he killed Dolly. I wondered if he had looked like that while he watched me thrashing in the middle of the pool.

"Get up, Joe."

Ellen flung an arm across his shoulder. "Joe, you promised last night, you ..."

He sat up and almost knocked her arm away. "I've had a bellyful of this guy."

He got to his feet with his athlete's grace and I took a step back and to the side, so I would not be between him and the pool. After all the years of vague enmity, all the months of wondering, all the days and nights of tortured conjecture, I was facing him. In a matter of moments, it would all be over. It had taken a lifetime, but that lifetime was ended. It was queer to watch it go away.

Ellen was sitting up, alarm and anger on her face.

"George, go call the police. George, do something, don't just sit there. George!"

"Well, what is it?" Joe said. He spat the words at me. "What do you want with me, Frank?"

"What can I do?" George said.

"Well, do *some*thing, don't just sit there!"

"Here's what I want," I said. "Was Dolly alive when you left her that night? That's all I want to know."

He was too angry to want to box with me. He threw a roundhouse right toward my chin. He wound up like a pitcher and I saw it coming from far behind his shoulder. I almost laughed out loud. It would be easy to block. A cinch. Joe was going to be easy pickings if that was the best he could do. First I would block this silly roundhouse and then he would be wide open and then I would ...

Something exploded against my jaw. Red came up out of the ground and went into my eyes and looked back out of them and I staggered and went down. I went down slowly, watching the world topple past in a great half circle. It was colored red but when I hit the flagstones it went black and then it looked natural again.

I looked up, spitting something out of my mouth. They were lined up, looking down at me. Joe's face—drawn, rigid, throbbing with blood—was in the center; on one side of it there were Maggie's inquisitive features and on the other side there was Ellen's slyly triumphant smile.

"Christ," George said. His head moved like a huge cabbage between Maggie's and Joe's. "You fetched him a good one that go-round." He peered down at me, nearsighted and owl-eyed without his glasses.

I shook my head and began to stand up. My reflexes were not as fast as they had been. That was the only explanation. In that brawl at Sasebo, I had taken on two Marine officers who would have eaten Joe for breakfast. It had taken a Colombian with a beer bottle to lay me out. The Colombian was just a little fellow but he was standing on a table.

Halfway up, crouched like a dog, I sprang forward and drove my shoulder against Joe's legs. Ellen screamed and I heard a hoarse grunt. That did it, I thought, that ...

A weight came down crushingly between my shoulder blades and I pitched forward. Somehow Joe's legs had got away from me. Wrong, I thought. All wrong here.

I was lying face down on the flagstones. They were hot against the skin of my face. My head ached horribly. I got up, swaying. My reflexes had certainly slowed down. But Christ, I'd been in the hospital, hadn't I?

"Joe? Where are you?" All I could see was red.

His hand touched my shoulder, spun me around. The red went away and I could see him plainly. His face looked small, like the face on a shrunken head from Borneo. Ensign Langley had had a shrunken head from Borneo. He hung it from the light over the mess table and it swung with the motion of the ship. You could get seasick as hell watching that head swing.

"You want to know anything else?" Joe said. "You want to hear more, Frank?"

Someone smaller than I was got in between us and pushed at me. It smelled like a woman and I looked down and my chin buried itself in hair. I pushed Ann away. "Frank!" I heard her cry, and someone grabbed at my arm and I pushed whoever that was away too and then I feinted with my left the way they had taught me during the war. At the same time I ducked and drove a jab toward his body, moving into position to cross my right to his jaw when he dropped his guard.

There was a loud noise in my ear. So they were shooting more rockets. That was all right, because this was the Fourth of July. This one went up and up and up. I watched it begin to come down. It picked up speed at thirty-two feet per second. At that rate it was moving quite swiftly when it struck me in the face. I was flat on my back and my face made a good target.

"Has he had enough?" I heard Joe say. "Does he want more?"

I tried to get up. Then I saw a face move down close over me in a great descending circle so that it started far above me looking like a shrunken head from Borneo and ended inches from my own head looking as huge and long as a mule's.

"Are you satisfied?" the mule's head said. "Does that answer your damned questions?"

I stared up at Joe. His skin glistened with sweat. Past him I could see George standing open-mouthed beside Ellen, who was tall and thin and straight against the hot blue sky, across which one white cloud drifted like cotton candy.

"I'm going to tell you something about Dolly." His voice rushed into the space between his head and mine. "You made her miserable for four years and then you come back here and accuse *me* of hurting her. When I loved her before she even knew you were alive. Loved her like you never knew how."

Someone shouted. People were running across the lawn toward the pool. I could hear the heavy footsteps.

"She never loved you worth a damn," Joe said. "She was just too chickenhearted to tell you so."

"What the devil is this?" Harry shouted.

Maggie's voice said something I couldn't make out.

"Everything's all right," Ellen said. Her voice was clear. I could hear it perfectly. I could hear Joe, too.

"That's why she's dead, do you hear me, Frank? Dolly's dead because she couldn't face your coming back."

"Cut that out," Harry said. "And get away from him, Joe."

"Aren't you proud?" Ann said. "You big strong man."

"Well, he started it, you saw him."

"He's *sick*. Can't you see he's sick?"

"He killed her," Joe said. "I can see that. He just as good as killed her, him and his big talk that I did it."

The shrunken head from Borneo was gone and George's open mouth was gone and the sly triumphant grin was gone but the cotton candy was still there and the sky was as blue as ever, even with the red between me and it. There were tears streaking Ann's face, and beside it now, staring down in fascination, Maggie's face wavered and blurred.

"I told you to take it easy," Walter was saying to me. His voice was gentle and so were his hands on my face. "Now look what you've gone and done."

But I was trying to hear Joe. What was that he had said? What was that incredible thing he had said?

"Dolly's dead because she couldn't face your coming back."

"Dolly," I said. "Dolly?"

But it became too dark too rapidly to remember any more. It became dark and I was alone with her.

"It's going to be different," Dolly said. "You wait and see when you come back, you just wait, Frank."

She was standing on the platform of Huntsville's decrepit little railroad station. A scalding summer wind swept her thin skirt hard against her legs. She held a wide-brimmed straw hat on the back of her head and from it a long baby-blue ribbon streamed out, fluttering. There were tears in her eyes, and when I kissed her, after two years, her lips still tasted as freshly of cherries as they had the night I first touched them with my own, in the days before Leander and the Cadillac and the symphonies and the hours of brooding silence.

"If it's just as good," I said, "that's all I'll ever ask of you, Dolly. Let me come back and find things just as good."

It was August of 1950. The Korean war had meant little to me until I received orders from the Naval Reserve. Even now, it seemed fantastic that I was catching a train for a reorientation school on the West Coast, from where I would be sent to the Far East.

"You ought not to ever come back," she said. "I wouldn't blame you if you didn't, Frank."

I took both of her hands in mine, looking past her at the ugly stores, the sun-baked streets of this poor dingy section of Huntsville. No one but Dolly had come to see me off. The people at the power company had given me a testimonial dinner the night before, but that was all. Harry had planned to come but had phoned his good-by instead; one of his colts was sick and he didn't feel he could leave. No one else had cared enough even to telephone. I had reached an armed and cautious truce with Huntsville, even with Belle and Mrs. Barnes, and its people no longer believed that I would make off with the Thompson fortune—although perhaps, someday, with the dime-store girl. The people I met at Old Hundred and at the Club had come to accord me a grudging and unenthusiastic place as an apparently unshakable addition to their set, so that, whether they liked it or not, and none of them would have if they had thought about it, they were also coming to an equally grudging and unenthusiastic acceptance of me as a person. Even so, they looked upon my Navy orders as a sort of poetic justice. The Far East was close enough to Siberia.

"I'm coming back, Dolly. I don't care about any of them. You know that. If you'll have me, I'm coming back."

She threw herself against me. Her soft arms went hard around my neck. Her whole body pressed into me and out of that pressure I called up for no reason at all the memory of our wedding night. We had stopped at a motel somewhere on the road to Florida, one of those antiseptic modern places where they leave everything wrapped in cellophane and you feel guilty if you drop a razor-blade wrapper in the gleaming wastebasket, and in the night I had got out of bed and stood naked by the window, feeling the air cool and light on my flesh, thinking rationally for the first time since we had driven laughing out of Huntsville, thinking what perhaps all bridegrooms think on their wedding night, that now, *now* I would show them, I would show the whole world, because I had something to work for. I had turned to look at her, thinking she was asleep, and had seen her looking at me, too, her great blue eyes at once trusting and faintly bewildered, and, compelled, I had gone across the room and swept her from the bed, swept her small white naked warm body close against mine, feeling the throb of blood under her skin, smelling the delicious feminine scent of her hair, thinking, I'll take care of you, I won't let anything happen to you never never never ...

I closed my eyes tightly against the hot thrust of that memory. It was so real I could feel the smooth cold tile under my feet again and hear the faint whirr of the air-conditioning system and smell the tinge of antiseptic in the air. Then I opened my eyes to the brilliant sun and the drab platform and the Negro porter watching gape-mouthed and I saw her wide straw hat go looping with the wind down the platform, felt the soft golden curl of her hair against my cheek.

"Frank," she whispered through three hard sobs that racked her body like coughs. "Frank, I've been so awful to you and I never meant it ... I never meant it ...."

"Everything's been as much my fault as yours," I said. "You never should have married me, I know that now."

"But I *wanted* you."

"I tried to make you happy, Dolly, I never wanted anything else."

"You did," she whispered. "It was just that sometimes I didn't know what I wanted any more, Frank, that was all."

But I had known too much of that sadness in her. It had been as much a part of her wide lovely eyes as their pupils. I had felt it in the bittersweet air that lurked about her like the faint aching scent of her perfume. It was plain on those long Sunday after-noons when the great thunder of the symphonies rolled out from the Stromberg-Carlson like all the combined voices of life and death and beauty and love and she would sit as if mesmerized by it, unspeaking, unmoving, hardly even breathing, the white fragile skin of her face luminescent in the growing darkness. It was in the constant play of her hands on Leander, the weightless touch of her breath on my neck, the murmuring voice, huskier now than when I had first known her, than in that long-ago time when I had walked the streets of Huntsville at night and dreamed of adding my voice to those that droned pleasantly and with such eternal ease beyond the wide lawns and the stone bird baths and the verbena-lined walks.

There had been no quarrels; I could never quarrel with Dolly. But often I would come home and find her gone to Old Hundred. The first time it happened, she was back in an hour; the last time, she stayed nearly a month. There was never anyone else, I knew that, even though Joe Spencer always tried to take advantage of these separations. It was simply that there would invariably come a time—I knew this, too, even though she refused ever to discuss her absences, even though she would sit in huddled and miser-able silence, clutching Leander, while my vain questions lost themselves in the booming music that so often now was like a third, unwelcome presence—a time when something in her cried out for Old Hundred, for everything it stood for, everything that existed nowhere else, everything she had sacrificed when she chose me.

"I want you to know I tried," I said. "I tried to be what you wanted, to live up to what you had a right to expect from me. I never let you down on purpose."

"Oh, Frank, don't! Don't *say* that!"

But I had to say it. Anybody else, I thought, any other man, could have done it, could have fitted in. Anybody else would have made friends, learned the way to do things, how to talk to people, at least how to ride a goddamned horse. Any other man but me could even have learned to get along with Ellen.

Yet I had never questioned that Dolly loved me and, as those years fell agonizingly behind, my own love had sharpened into a sort of complete adoration that, day by day, had sapped steadily and alarmingly at my own vitality, my own identity. Sometimes, in the long summer-scented nights, I dreamed I found the same ecstasy I had seen in her face that first night, that ecstasy I had known her then to be capable not only of inspiring, but of experiencing, too. I dreamed I found it, but I never did; and in the cold hopeless mornings it seemed more elusive, more desperately impossible than before, simply because it had been so near.

The train came in with a rush and a snort, making Huntsville's once-a-day connection with the outside world. It stopped with a terrible grind and clatter and I looked up and thought that nothing in the world had ever been so bleak and forbidding and lonely as the soiled green baize of those empty seats in that grimy coach that would take me away from her.

"Frank," she whispered against me, "you take care of yourself."

I pushed her away and swung my Val-Pak aboard.

"Us bad pennies," I said. "We always turn up."

For a long time after the train pulled out, she wrote me later, she stood looking after it, hardly able to believe I was gone so quickly. "I wanted you back so much. I wanted us to start all over, maybe be different people. Me especially."

There was no observation platform on that sorry train, so I could not look back. I could carry with me, though, the memory of her thin lovely body outlined in the wind and the wide silvery blue of her eyes and her voice whispering, whispering as it always had in those dreams in which, in spite of everything, we had approached the earthly immortality of love.

CHAPTER EIGHT

"WHAT WE WANT to be sure to do," Walter said, "is to make him talk right away."

I could feel his hands working at a bandage on my head. The spot under it on my scalp tingled and itched, so that I knew it had been shaved. I came wide awake while he was talking. There were others moving in the room, but I kept my eyes shut; I would have to face them soon enough.

"If Joe really hurt him," Harry said, "I mean if he causes him to have a relapse or something, I'll run him off the place, damn if I won't."

"Don't blame Joe too much. Frank practically accused him of doing something to Dolly," Maggie said.

"Joe knows the shape he's in. We were talking about it this morning at Possum Lake."

"Possum Lake?" Walter said. "Did yall go fishing without me?"

"Didn't think you'd want to go so early. Anyway, we didn't get a bite. Got back here at dawn."

"I was so upset," Maggie said, as if they had not even spoken. "I saw all that blood coming out of Frank's head and there was Joe looking like a wild man and it's a wonder I didn't jump in the pool or something."

"It's a good thing Ann ran for Harry and me," Walter said. "You and George and Ellen were doing a fat lot of good standing around with your big mouths hanging open."

Fishing at Possum Lake, I thought. Joe and Harry fishing at Possum Lake and coming back at dawn. Then Joe couldn't have …

"He's going to be all right, isn't he, Walter?" Harry said.

"He'll be O.K. physically," Walter said. "The thing to worry about is whether all those things Joe said and the shock of getting kicked around like that drop him off the deep end again."

"It's hard to imagine that. I mean Frank … crazy."

"That's a strong word."

Walter's hands put the final touch on the bandage. I could smell his pipe tobacco; it was warm and comforting, the way the baths used to be, and I let it drift down into my lungs and held it there a moment, not breathing at all.

"Frank had a tremendous shock out there in the war somewhere. I only know a little bit about it, but from the word the Navy sent me from Philadelphia, I gather Frank fouled up and somebody got killed. Those things happen in a war. But you know what a sensitive guy he's always been. He used to blame himself every time Dolly had a stomachache."

I let the smoke float gently out of my chest. Dolly had had monster stomachaches at least twice a week. She would never admit that old-fashioned gas caused them.

"Do you remember how he'd stand on the edge of the dance floor out at the Club and watch her getting a big rush?" Walter said. "Not like he was jealous. Like he wanted to make sure she was having a good time. Maybe in spite of him."

"Cut it out," Harry said. He cleared his throat. "Do you think there's really any danger this time, Walt?"

I was lying on a leather sofa, my feet propped up on one armrest. It must have been in Harry's den, and I knew if I opened my eyes I would be staring right up at the empty spot on the mantel where the china dog had stood for so long.

"The other time he was completely worn out, Harry. He'd had nearly two years of war and strain and fear and he was on edge because he was almost through with it."

"He's on edge now, too."

"Sure. But on top of all that, he didn't crack the other time until he was informed about Dolly. The Navy told me that. That's what they thought did the real dirty work, on top of everything else. I'm not a psychiatrist, but it doesn't take one to figure it all out."

"Blamed himself," Harry said. "Christ, I guess none of us ever gave the guy much of a hand, did we?"

"He ought to be O.K.," Walter said. "He'll come around any minute, and if he'll just talk right off he'll be O.K."

"Why so?"

"Like I said a minute ago, Frank was never really crazy. He had just had this tremendous shock, like a mental earthquake. It didn't do much damage to amount to anything, but it broke a couple of wires here and there. Until something mended them, Frank couldn't talk."

It doesn't sound so terrible the way Walter tells it, does it?

Frank couldn't talk. Lots of worse things than that. You can write things down or learn a sign language or something. But what if you can't? What if you can't do those things, either?

What if the trouble is not so much that you can't talk—although you certainly can't, although your lips are thick and clumsy and you can feel the skin of your throat lying in old dead folds across what was once a larynx? What if that's not it so much as that you can't communicate at all?

"Maybe that's when you really go crazy," I said. I opened my eyes and my voice cracked in the middle of "really."

"You damned eavesdropper," Walter said. "When is when you really go crazy?"

"When you can't make yourself understood. You wouldn't know, Walter."

I sat up, bracing my neck, moving slowly, the blood that had gone to my head beginning to drain slowly down so that I had the queerest feeling of slow flowing, of being lost somewhere between solid and liquid.

"Frank," Harry said. "Take it easy, boy."

He was leaning forward in the leather chair, his elbows on his knees, his hands clasped in front of him. He was smiling and there were relief and understanding in his face. I thought they made it softer and younger; he was a strikingly handsome man and he had a look of pride and confidence and courage. From him I took some of those things myself, although, God knows, I had little enough reason to feel any of them.

"Well," I said, "by God, I guess he hit me with the ring post, didn't he?"

"No," Walter said, "but if there had been one handy I expect he might have."

"The ... ah ... the hospital. I guess I was weaker than I thought I was."

"Sure," Harry said. "Hell, you must be thirty pounds lighter than you used to be."

"You can't lose weight like that and stay in shape, can you?"

"Listen," Harry said, "you're not supposed to worry about all that from now on. You understand? You're just going to take it easy and lie out there by the pool and put that weight back on. O.K.?"

Once, months before, I had been sitting in a warm bath and the water had been moving in slow whirls around me. It was so good and so close, like the slow luxurious press of a woman's body; but suddenly I was weeping. It had become intolerable to feel so good and to have no way to make anyone understand, to have no one to make understand if there had been a way.

Now I knew that if there had been someone and some way, I might have wept anyway. Tears scalded the underside of my eyelids and I had to hold them back with a shake of my head.

"Why, goddamn it," Harry said, "you belong here. I don't know why we never realized all that a long time ago."

The feeling of flow was gone as abruptly as if it had been a thought I could dismiss. Harry had said I belonged at Old

Hundred—Harry Thompson, who reigned benevolently where I had so long been an undesirable alien; Harry, in whose veins the old proud blood truly flowed, in whose heart the old proud way of life was truly preserved; who should have been, so Dolly had said, with Jackson at Chancellorsville or Longstreet at Chickamauga; who perhaps, in that blood and that heart and that tradition, actually had been at one of those places, just as Dolly had wished for him.

"You look funny," Harry said.

"I'm fine. But ... I guess I've been pretty much of a louse."

He stood up, waving a hand airily. "Which would you rather do, sleep or eat? Right now, I mean."

"I'll stay here a while and snooze. P.B. can fix me a sandwich later."

They went out, looking, I thought, vastly relieved. It became quiet in Harry's den. I stretched out, staring at the empty shelf where the ugly china dog had stood so incongruously. I tried to think about Joe, about what I could do or say now, but I started to doze. From somewhere in the yard, I could hear voices talking, the words merging into one great drowsy murmur. The fog came down then and I slept. I had a horrid dream in which people stood around me and smiled ghoulishly and pointed with skeleton fingers to a spot just beside me. I finally turned my head and there lay Dolly; and the blood all around her flowed together and formed the word "REPENT" in big staggering capitals.

I woke up, my mouth tasting evilly of fear and thirst and the churning vapors of my stomach. My head pounded wildly. I sat up carefully, holding it in my hands. My jaw was lumpy where Joe had hit me. Pretty soon my eyes focused on Ellen. She was sitting in the leather chair. She wore a thin print dress with a prim collar and big pockets and her slender legs were bare and crossed.

I had the feeling she had been looking at me for a long time. Her eyes were for a moment fixed and almost glassy, before we both moved. A small shudder of distaste went up my spine at the thought of her sitting there watching with her cold eyes while I slept.

"I guess I look like what the cat dragged in," I said.

"Your head is bleeding again. You'd better find Walter."

"I can stand it if you can."

She nodded, slowly, looking again at my bleeding head, my smeared and wrinkled shirt.

"I've talked to Harry," she said. "He seems to have acted against my advice."

"Oh?"

"I told him this morning that I felt everyone would be better off if you … went away. Now it seems he's told you you're to stay as long as you want."

"So you don't want to be friends any more. Not like last night."

"You won't let anybody be your friend. You won't act decently."

I laughed. "You want me to take my meals in the kitchen with P.B. and Easter?"

"That will be all right about that," she said, as if my proposal had been serious. "I just want to tell you that I can put up with a lot, but that I won't stand for your being unpleasant to Joe or anybody else again."

"He was a bit unpleasant himself." I put my hand on my head.

"He loved her for so long, Joe did. And then you said all those things to him. I don't blame him for what he did to you."

"Neither do I."

"Even when he was a little boy he loved her. He used to come out and give her rides on his bicycle. And you said he killed her."

"All right," I said. "All *right*. I said I was wrong, didn't I? You want me to write it on the blackboard a hundred times?"

"It wasn't as if you had any right. It wasn't as if Dolly ever loved you, really loved you."

My body went rigid on the sticky sweating leather of the sofa.

"That's a lie, Ellen. He said that, too, but it's a lie. I ought to know if she loved me."

The faintest suggestion of a smile hovered on her lips and was gone.

"You were too much in love yourself. You never knew. You thought because…" She stopped, and something, not a smile, twitched at her lips and went away again. "You thought she loved you."

"Because what?" I was suddenly furious. They keep saying it and saying it, I thought. She *did* love me, Dolly did.

"Because what?" I said again. "Make it plain, Ellen."

"Because she…loved somebody," Ellen said, "you thought it was you. All those years you thought it was you."

Each word fell on my ear with a hollow and echoing boom.

"You're welcome to stay as long as you like. Just like Harry told you."

She stood up and went across the room and out without looking back.

"Lies," I muttered. Then, *"Lies!"* I yelled at the forbidding door, at the fixed repellent image of her going toward it.

Hadn't I known Dolly better than any of them? Hadn't I been with her in sickness and in health, for richer and for poorer? Hadn't I spent four long years loving her? Hadn't I held her in the weeping nights, carried in my heart the image of her delicate brooding face and her white skin and her little body, forever running down the lawn from the great white house toward me?

Oh, I had known Dolly better than any of them. Not so long, perhaps, but she had told me of the years before I came to Huntsville and I had known her then, too, perhaps in spirit better than any of them had known her in actuality. The only way they had really seen her that I hadn't was dead.

Perhaps not even that way. Because there had been a day at Philadelphia when I had been in the doctor's office and he had been called to the phone in another room. I had been left alone to wait for him because I was known to be harmless, even docile. I got up and began to wander aimlessly about the office. Finally I stood behind his desk. I could see a name neatly typed on the tab of a file folder: "SINCLAIR, Franklin J., Lt, 44682/1105, USNR." Beneath some kind of form on top of the papers in the folder I saw the edge of a glossy photograph. I pulled the photograph out of the folder and took a step toward the window for better light.

It was a photograph of an automobile smashed against a huge boulder. The metal was incredibly twisted and torn and thrust about. It was difficult even to tell what kind of car it had been. But I knew. I knew what car that was without turning the picture over and reading the information typed on the back, without looking even at the lone pitiful hand shown hanging limp and dead from one crushed door. I knew all about the picture.

I looked up and the doctor was standing in the door, waiting for me to move or react. I spoke for the first time in eight months.

"Dolly didn't do this."

Speaking was like going home, but now home was no good; home was terrifying and ugly, like the picture.

"Dolly wouldn't have made anything so ugly. Not on purpose. Dolly hated ugly things."

But that had been four months ago. It had been easy then to make up my mind that someone had killed her. I had not yet come back to Old Hundred and seen the casual acceptance of Dolly as a suicide; I had not seen the fierce anger in Joe Spencer's eyes; I had not heard his furious voice whispering, "She never loved you worth a damn," and I had not heard Ellen say, "All those years you thought it was you."

It was stifling hot. I could see the sun's rays slanting in through the window and the motes of dust hanging motionless in them. Perspiration was breaking hotly out all over me and my damp shirt clung stickily under my arms, between my shoulder blades. My mouth was open and I was sucking the thick warm air in fishlike gasps.

I couldn't stand it in there. I took two long staggering strides to the door and hurled it open, hearing it go all the way around on its staid old hinges and smack hard against the wall. Then I was plunging down the quiet hallway, watching the wide floor boards lurch gleaming beneath my shoes. I swung around the newel post and lunged at the stairs, throwing myself past the landing where Harry had put the grandfather clock in place of the portrait of Dolly's mother. Then I was on the second floor with a new hall narrowing in front of me and down that hall was the high old room and the canopied bed and then I was sinking down into something deep and warm like the baths had been, and revolving, too, in the same slow warm soothing way the green chlorinated water had whirled and gurgled past me.

The sharp spines of a mine showed suddenly evil in the water. My body went rigid. I rolled over and lay on my back. Dish towels began to float down in regular pendulous swoops, going by me gently. I could hear the great gloomy sonorities of the symphonies. Out of the midst of the floating pendulous dish towels a long blue ribbon streamed undulant in a summer wind. Then the wind began to blow harder, tearing at the ribbon. The slap and pop of its lashing end became like the slap and pop of a twenty-millimeter mount letting go. Dish towels fell one by one while I listened to the Stromberg-Carlson and the great sonorities and the intolerable ache of the lonely whistle blowing. The face of Dolly was beside me; it was the face of death, and while I watched it the great sonorities took on the sound of death and the dish towels began to swerve and go past, farther down. I could look after them down to where they disappeared. The Stromberg-Carlson no longer spoke in the vast sonorities of the symphonies, but in whispers brushing dryly. They reminded me of death and the rotting stench of cherries. I leaned over the edge, looking after the towels. It was so dark .... Then the slide began. It was irresistible.

Something long and powerful went around my shoulders and held tight. Something else went around my head. I was pulled forward until there was a softness under my head. It rose and fell and a cool, soothing thing began to move on the sticky skin of my face.

"What's the matter, Frank?"

Those arms—that was what they were, warm, softly fleshed arms, bare to the shoulder—had caught me on the edge of the pit. But the dark was still there; I knew that. It was still there, still waiting for me if I looked at it. The minute I began to look at it again I would go over. They couldn't go on catching me forever.

"Why didn't you let me?" I said. "Why did you stop me?"

"You were having a nightmare, Frank."

"Nightmare?" My head was lying against a woman's breast and the voice was a woman's and the hands were unmistakably feminine.

"Ann?"

"Yes?" Something cool and wet touched my forehead.

"Let me hold you like this."

"All right."

"You ought to have let me go over."

"Go over? I couldn't let you lie here and twist and groan the way you were."

"Now you've stopped me, you've got to help me, too."

"You're going to be all right. You just hold me like that a minute."

"I'm scared."

"Scared? What on earth of?"

"It's so *dark* down there. It swirls around."

"Don't think about it now."

"I don't want to be crazy, Ann. Don't let me be crazy again."

"I don't think you ever were."

"But don't you see I've got to find out or I will be again?"

"Find out *what?*"

It was getting hot again. My eyes were closed and it was dark, but not so dark as it had been down there.

"Find out if she did it. If she did, I'll have to go back down there."

"Frank! Stop this now and go to sleep."

"Because if she killed herself it was because of me."

Ann took her arms from around me. The softness went away and the bed creaked as she stood up.

"Let's stop this foolishness, Frank. Get up."

"What?" I opened my eyes.

"I said get up from there. Stop acting as if somebody's stolen your toys."

She was standing by the bed with her hands on her hips, staring down at me. There was a small frown on her face and she was biting her lower lip in annoyance.

"If somebody pushed you into the pool, somebody killed Dolly. That's what you thought this morning, at least."

I sat up and swung my legs over the side of the bed. My head was light and bouncy and I almost went over on my face. She was standing wide-legged, one toe lightly tapping the floor. She was wearing high heels and stockings.

"Everybody has nightmares," she said. "I ought to know. But I can't stand to see a man carry on like a child. If you think somebody killed Dolly, why don't you call the police? If you don't, shut up about it."

"You go to hell," I said. "What right have you got to talk to me like that?"

"The same right you had to say the things you said to me this morning. If you don't like it, *you* go to hell!"

She turned and took a quick stride or two toward the door. The tight skirt of her white linen dress brushed against my legs.

She was wearing a little white hat, too, and she was holding her head up stiffly. Every line of her was taut with outrage.

"Wait a minute," I said. "Don't go away mad."

"I'm not mad. You just make me so *tired!* But she stopped, looking back at me. Her arms, in the sleeveless dress, were tanned and slender. I had never seen her look so well, I thought; anger became her. Maybe she should get mad more often.

"Why so dressed up?" I tried to sound pleasant. It had become for some reason quite important that we should part friends.

She looked down at herself, smoothing an invisible wrinkle over her thigh.

"It's the Fourth of July. You know, they always have that VFW thing."

Every Independence Day, the William R. Harold Post of the Veterans of Foreign Wars marched to the monument they had erected to Billy Harold on the courthouse lawn and placed a wreath there. I had forgotten about it, although it had been tradition even before I had left.

"You look mighty pretty," I said. "I'm sorry I ... annoyed you. I really am."

"That's all right, Frank. I know you ... I mean ... I spoke pretty sharply, I guess."

"Listen," I said. "Listen, Ann ..." There was something very important to be said. I could not quite think what it was. She turned all the way back to face me. She wore hardly any lipstick and her lips were slightly parted so that I could see her even white teeth. I had never realized how good-looking Ann Harold was. Always before I had only felt vaguely sorry for her.

"Why don't I go with you?" I said.

"Why, that ... Do you want to?"

I stood up. My head was feeling much better but I knew I looked horrible. I had not minded before, but now I was embarrassed.

"Give me five minutes. You won't know me."

She smiled then. Her lips curved beautifully and it made me feel good to see it. A smile became her, too, just like anger.

"I'll wait in my car. It's out front."

She turned and went out. When the door closed behind her, I realized I was smiling, too, widely and foolishly, and that I never had said to her whatever it was that had seemed important.

CHAPTER NINE

HAD NEEDED to be told off, I thought, while I made myself as presentable as possible; nothing is so disgusting as someone wallowing around in self-pity. I hadn't needed Ellen's sly insinuations or Joe's shouted accusations, but I had needed Ann's common sense. That had put things in proper focus again.

I went downstairs almost blithely. After all, it was a lovely day. There was a pretty girl waiting for me in a luxurious car. I was a free man, resasonably healthy. The ache in my head and the drawing, burning sensation where my scalp had been shaved and the cut treated were hardly noticeable now. And the things Joe and Ellen had said were faint and almost indistinguishable, merely parts of some absurd long-ago dream.

Maggie was just coming in from the front porch. She wore a sun dress from which her broad tanned shoulders and the huge slopes of her breasts rose massively. The dress was too young for her. She was smiling in some secret triumph, as if she had caught little boys in the garage doing something they shouldn't.

"Are you really going with Ann?" she said.

I could even feel cheerful with Maggie. I stopped and looked over her bosom as she expected me to do.

"Unless she's left me. Three's a crowd or I'd say come with us."

"Oh, she hasn't left. Not that girl. She's out there holding her breath for fear you'll change your mind."

"I better go before she turns blue, then."

I went past Maggie and out on the front porch. It was still early afternoon and the sun was high and hot. It was a brilliant day and the light reflected sharply from Ann's polished Lincoln, where it waited in the drive.

"Sorry to keep you waiting." I climbed into the front seat beside her. "Had to powder my nose."

"I didn't mind."

The car moved slowly away. It was big and powerful and silent and just to ride in it helped a man relax. I stretched my legs in front of me and sighed in the first real comfort I had known in a long time. There was an open carton of cigarettes on the seat beside me.

"Thirty miles an hour, McGillicuddy," I said. "And we'll take the turnpike, if you please. No sudden stops."

"Yes, *sir!*" Ann smiled at me, a nice wide friendly smile. It was absurd how good I felt. A half hour before I had been floundering like a wounded buffalo. That morning I had deliberately gone out and forced a fist fight. Now, hot as it was, I could almost imagine it to be one of those green fresh early-spring days when everyone is smiling.

Ann was a smooth driver. The Lincoln flashed past the big rock with its letters spelling "REPENT" before I was even aware of it. The cigarettes slid against my leg and I pushed them away.

"I'll tell you what," I said. "Let's drive to Florida. The hell with those scrounges back at Old Hundred."

"Why Florida? It's too hot down there in July. Let's go to the mountains."

"Right. Rent us a cabin somewhere and go fishing. Do you like to fish, Ann?"

"I don't know. I've never been."

"You don't know what you've been missing. There's something about fishing that puts a man right with himself. It doesn't matter whether you catch anything or not. It's something else."

"I always get to thinking about the worms. I think I'd like fishing and then I get to thinking about the worms you have to stick on the hook and somehow I never go."

"Who's talking about worms?" I said. "This day and time you can buy lures and things and never see a worm."

"Anyway," Ann said, "I don't guess I can go."

"The hell with what people will say. We'll hang a blanket down the middle of the cabin. If they believe Clark Gable stayed on his side in that movie, they'll believe I did."

"It's not that. It's just that …"

She stopped and I remembered where we were actually going.

"I'm sorry," I said. "I wasn't thinking."

"Oh, that's all right."

"It was such a nice day and somehow I got to feeling so good I forgot."

"Never mind it," Ann said. "It doesn't bother me to think about Billy. He's been dead nearly ten years now."

Nine, I thought. Nine, to be exact. Nine times you've had to go down there in public and stand there with everybody looking at you and listen to them rake it all up again.

"I don't suppose it's much fun for you," I said.

She shrugged. Her face became fixed and stiff.

"I'm all that's left of the Harold family, Frank. We were a tradition in this town and they expect me to carry it on. I don't suppose it's too much to ask."

"Other people were killed, you know."

"But Billy was the youngest." She swung the car expertly into the main highway, merging with the heavy holiday traffic. "And he came from the best family. There wasn't any argument at all about who the VFW would name their post for and build that awful monument to."

No, I thought, not after you made a contribution toward building their clubhouse, there wasn't.

"I don't know," Ann said. "I don't like ceremonies. I don't like having to listen to the same pious eulogy every year and I can't *stand* for them to act like I'm a widow or something, but they expect it of me. I suppose the family would too. I don't know anything I can do about it."

"You're your own boss, aren't you?"

"Yes, but ... I guess you couldn't understand. It's just that *I'm* the family now, Frank, I'm all there is left of it, and they *expect* me to ... be what the family's always been. I know it sounds funny."

But it didn't. It made too much sense. It explained too many things. Of course, she wasn't her own boss. Huntsville was her boss, Huntsville with its powerful archaic conception of things as they should be, not of things as they were. In Huntsville, acceptance demanded conformity. For Ann, conformity might mean a different thing entirely from what it had meant for me, but it was still the basic requirement. And Ann had been brought up to meet it.

"It's ironic, though," she said. "There was a boy who worked at the bank, long before you ever came to town. He was a good, smart boy, about my age, and he worked hard. Only he came from a poor family down on Cedar Street and his father couldn't keep a job. He fought all through the war, not just in one battle. And most people don't even remember that he was killed too— three days after Billy was."

We were coming into Huntsville now. There was a big sign at the city limits that read: "We Love Our Children—Drive Slowly."

"But they named the post for Billy. And built a monument to him on the courthouse lawn. And do you know what he was doing the last time I saw him?"

"Look," I said. "I didn't mean to get all this started."

"He was crawling up the front steps of our house, vomiting," Ann said. "He was so drunk he didn't even know what was going on. That was the night before he went in the Army, but he was that way every night from the time he was seventeen. Oh, he was a sweet kid, Billy was."

"Now let's drop this cheerful conversation," I said. "I didn't mean to get all this started just because I thought about going to Florida."

She laughed and I saw the fixed edged lines disappear from her face.

"I believe you'd really go if I said yes," she said. "You don't know what you'd be letting yourself in for." She swung the car into Sycamore Street, under the thick canopy of interlaced trees that would shade us all the way to the courthouse. The cigarette carton slid against my leg again.

"Sure I do." I picked up the cigarettes and pushed the button on the glove compartment. "What able-bodied man wouldn't take off for Florida in a Lincoln with a rich and well-stacked blonde?"

She laughed again, tossing her head back a little. "You make me sound like something from Hollywood. Am I really a well-stacked blonde?"

But I wasn't listening. I was staring into the glove-compartment, at the pint of bourbon lying on its side. It was a little over half empty. It was very good bourbon. It would have cost a hell of a lot at the ABC store over in the next county.

I took the bottle out of the glove compartment.

"All this and fire water, too. We're really going to have a ball in Florida, aren't we?"

She snatched the bottle from my hand and almost threw it back into the glove compartment. The car lurched and straightened. But she had been close to me long enough for me to smell bourbon on her breath. She must have taken a bracer while she was waiting in the car for me.

"All right," she said. "All *right*. You can just keep your big mouth shut about it! It's my business and you can just ... just ..."

Tears sparkled faintly in her eyes. Her lips worked spasmodically and she looked away from me. Then, with some hard, quick inner compulsion, she gained control of herself, so that those etched, rigid lines appeared about her mouth and nostrils again.

I didn't want to make any more wisecracks. I didn't want to say anything that would hurt her or make her feel worse. I didn't want to say anything like that, but I didn't know what I *did* want to say, either.

I touched her shoulder, awkwardly, from my position beside her.

"Ann, listen. I..."

"I don't want to talk about it, Frank." Her voice was an arid whisper. "I don't want to talk about anything right now."

I took my hand off her shoulder. Down the green tunnel of Sycamore Street I could see the crowd already waiting at the courthouse.

The parade was coming into the square from the opposite side. Ann parked in front of the Cut-Rate Drug Company and we watched the marchers spill out in confusion over the courthouse lawn, their long hike from the schoolhouse through the business district ended.

There were two high-school bands and there were not only the somewhat paunchy VFW marchers—most of them World War II vets—but also an even paunchier and more balding American Legion group—mostly World War I veterans. There were innumerable Boy and Girl Scout troops, and every store in town had entered a float.

It was a big parade. It marched about twenty blocks under a sun hot enough to kill off mules in the field, then gathered docilely on the courthouse lawn with the rest of the town to hear the speechmaking. There was nothing unusual about it. It happened just this way every Fourth of July. It even ended the same way, with the Daughters of the Confederacy striding pompously in the rear, waving the Stars and Bars as proudly as if they themselves had bled and suffered and died under them.

"We'd better go over," Ann said. "They always present the wreath before the main speech."

"Let us by all means avoid the main speech," I said. "Who's speaking?"

She opened her door. "You don't have to come at all, Frank. You can just sit here in the shade and ..."

I got out. The asphalt of the street was sticky under my feet. The sun hit me a solid lick on the back of the neck.

"Don't be silly," I said. I went around the car and held the door for her, then took her arm. We started across the street. While we were out in the middle one of the bands struck up "The Star-Spangled Banner" and there was a flag-raising ceremony. We had to stand quietly until that was over.

The monument to Private William R. Harold stood on the southeast corner of the square, diagonally opposite the Confederate monument. To its left there was a World War I monument. I wondered if they would take the remaining corner for a Korean monument or if they would wait for a "real" war to come along.

The Harold memorial was of an American infantryman who looked like Tyrone Power, not the pictures I had seen of Billy Harold. This figure lunged forward, bayonet at the ready, atop a ten-foot-high marble base. It was as still and unnatural as a leg in a cast and its face wore an expression of sublimity. Every year, on the third of July, two old Negroes came out and wiped the pigeon droppings off it. The rest of the year no one seemed to notice this indignity.

The plaque on the base read: "IN MEMORIAM—Private William R. Harold—Killed June 6, 1944, In Defense of Democracy—Our Finest Flower, He Gave His All."

They were still winding up the parade and getting the floats out of the way of traffic. When Ann and I reached the monument there were only a few others waiting for the wreath ceremony. They looked at us curiously, obviously wondering who the familiar-looking man was, but no one stood near enough to hear us.

"I hate that…that monstrosity," Ann said, looking at the monument to her brother. I looked it over closely. I had seen worse.

"I wouldn't call it art. But I don't see anything so awful about it."

"That look on the face. If you'd known Billy—he used to look that way, like an angel, after he'd shot a cat with a BB gun."

"For God's sake, Ann, let's get out of here. This is ghoulish."

She put her hand on my arm. It was steady. "I'm perfectly all right, Frank. I'm really quite used to this sort of thing by now."

The crowd was moving down to us. Gradually, people clustered about the monument, gaping first at it, then, invariably, at Ann, immaculate and cool-looking in her white dress. Feeling vaguely protective, I stood nearer her, but she moved a little aside, as if she did not want to be touched.

Finally, when the crowd had completely encircled the monument, when the close-pressed bodies had made the heat as stifling as it was burning, a small lane opened and a handsome, husky man came striding through it. He did not look as young as he once had, but his blue overseas cap, bearing the post name and number, sat jauntily on his head. He was carrying a huge funeral wreath; its ribbon read in silver letters, "July 4, 1953."

He was Wayne Bullock, a cousin of Ellen's, and the perennial commander of the VFW. He was big and hearty and stupid and he had been, according to Dolly, the first boy who had ever kissed her. It had been so disgusting, she said, that she had not let anybody else kiss her for the next two years.

Wayne came to Ann immediately. He looked at me without recognition—not surprising, since he had never spoken two words to me without being forced to. He took her hand and looked at her with eyes filled with dime-store sympathy.

"Good girl," he said. "I knew we could count on you to be here." I wondered if he had counted on the whisky on her breath.

Wayne went over to the base of the monument. Several other dignitaries had gathered there.

"Friends and fellow Americans," Wayne said. "This has always been an informal ceremony. We've come here to honor our friend Billy Harold every Fourth of July for a long time now, just the way he'd want us to—kind of informal and folksy-like."

Ann looked around at me, then quickly away. In her eyes I saw something almost wild, but trapped and dying.

"We know he was a great guy," Wayne said. "We know he died gladly for democracy, for you and me. We know he gave his life like he would have given us the shirt off his back if we'd of asked him for it. And we know he wouldn't want us to come here and make real fancy speeches over his memory."

I looked around at the crowd. They were staring at Wayne, nodding approvingly. They must have known Billy Harold. They must have known he wasn't any greater than a half-million others. They must have known that nobody dies gladly, and damn few die for democracy or anything else if they can help it. They must have known those things while they listened to Wayne Bullock drag out his platitudes.

"Now I'm going to ask Reverend John Jamieson to say a little prayer," Wayne said. "Yall know he was a chaplain in France and he knows what a sacrifice Billy Harold made. After that, I've got a little surprise in mind. Reverend?"

The Reverend Jamieson looked a little embarrassed at that introduction, but he said a nice short prayer. While I was standing with my head bowed, I felt Ann back up against me. She was as stiff and taut as the statue of her brother. I wondered what Wayne Bullock had in mind that would be a surprise.

"Thank you, Reverend," he said, when the prayer was ended. "Now, fellow Americans, I could stand up here and tell you about Billy Harold all day, but yall know the great story of what he did already. I know it by heart and so do you. It makes us all better men and women and better Americans to know it. But what we don't know is what a man like that was really like. I think on this day of commemoration we'd all like to know more about Billy Harold—not about the great thing he did, but the little things we all know he must have done. And before I lay this wreath humbly before his monument, I'm going to ask a mighty brave little girl to come up here and tell us those things—his sister, Ann."

He grinned stupidly and broadly and held out his hand to her. I could hear her breath suck in, so sharply I could imagine it burning along her throat and in her chest. That idiot, I thought, doesn't he have *any* sense?

Then I saw that great circle of staring expectant eyes on her. They wanted her to do it, too; they wanted her to get up there and tell them what a wonderful boy her brother had been, how he had helped his mother and honored his father and taken flowers to his first-grade teacher, how she knew he had been overjoyed to get his head blown off for democracy. They wanted her to tell them what they wanted to hear. They wanted her to be what they expected her to be.

Her elbow was touching my ribs. It trembled. She swayed forward and I knew she was going to do it. She was going to do what they all wanted, just as she had done all her life.

I took her arm in my hand and pulled her around. "I'll be *damned* if you will," I said.

I thrust my shoulder against the man standing behind me and he jumped hastily out of the way. A lane opened and I dragged her quickly through it toward the street.

"Frank! I can't… Let me…"

"Shut up!"

The crowd stumbled and fell back. Behind me it began to mutter and rumble, and I heard Wayne's startled angry bellow. Then we were through and, not looking back, I was running across and down the street toward the Lincoln, pulling her behind me. She was not resisting, but she was not helping me, either. And now the sound of the crowd behind us was loud and bewildered and outraged.

"Those idiots!" The two words ground between my clenched teeth. "Who the hell do they think they are? Who the hell—"

"Ann!" It was Wayne, running across the street after us, roaring like an offended corporal.

We were almost to the Lincoln. I dragged her the last few steps, opened the door, and stuffed her in like a rag doll. Then I ran around and got in under the wheel, slamming the door just as Wayne puffed up, followed by a few of the more curious from the monument crowd. Wayne was still carrying the wreath.

"What the devil is this?" he rumbled. "Ann, what—"

"Move it, General!" I pushed him back from the window and started the engine. "You'll get a tread mark on your foot in a second."

Hot blood turned his face a glowing red. He threw the wreath down on the pavement and grabbed the door handle. The car was already moving away from the curb, but he pulled open the door. I slammed on the brakes. The bastard, I thought. I'm going to have to hit him.

"Wayne," Ann said.

Her voice was quiet, so quiet I looked over my shoulder at her. She was sitting quite still and those deep sharp lines of control were plain about her mouth and nose. "You had no right to ask so much of me, Wayne."

"Right!" Wayne bellowed. "Are you a Harold or aren't you? Just tell—"

"You had no right," Ann said. "Frank, please. Let's go."

I slammed the door again. Wayne was too outraged and baffled to hold it open.

"You heard the lady," I said. I backed the Lincoln quickly out and drove down the street. The crowd around the monument looked at us in hostile silence. All right, I thought. Let them. We're not running for Congress.

It was cool and dark in the green tunnel of Sycamore Street and the proud old houses rose disapprovingly on both sides. I had the feeling there were a thousand eyes peering at us from each of them. I didn't even slow down at the far end, skidding the Lincoln out into the highway ahead of an approaching oil truck.

"I think," Ann said, "I know what I need." She punched the button of the glove compartment and the lid dropped open.

"Me too," I said. I took the bottle out of her hand and, steering with my knees, twisted the cap off. I lifted it and took a short drink. It was damn good whisky. Then I threw the bottle out the window. It almost hit the "We Love Our Children" sign.

"Nothing like a snort to pick you up," I said, and stepped down on the accelerator.

"All right," Ann said. "You seem to be the big boss around here so suppose you just drive this car right straight to Old Hundred and then get out of my sight just as quick as you can."

"My, my. Aren't we being a little bitter and sarcastic, everything considered?"

"*I'm* not sarcastic. And I'm certainly not bitter just because you're acting like Neanderthal man or whatever it is you think you are. I don't—"

"—care to talk about it. I know, I know. You're mighty cute when you stick your nose up in the air that way."

"That's no business of yours."

"Sure it is." I let the Lincoln slow down, then turned into the country road leading to Old Hundred. "Cute women are always a man's business."

"That's all you think about, isn't it? What you call cute women and your—"

I reached out backhanded and put my palm across her lips. "You're the first girl I ever saw get mad about being called cute. Or for being rescued from a wolf pack."

Her teeth sank into the skin of my hand, not hard. Over my thumb I could see her eyes flick toward me, then away. They were trying hard to be angry.

"Say," I said. "Did you see Wayne's face when we drove off?"

The teeth let go of my skin. The eyes flicked at me again and there was a muffled sound from under my head.

"That big sap," I said. "I always wanted to stick a pin in him and see how many pounds he'd lose."

The eyes were laughing now and I took my hand away and saw the rest of her face laughing too. She looked younger than I had ever seen her look before, almost like a little girl, laughing fully and freely with no inhibition at all.

"Oh, Frank! You've *ruined* me in Huntsville!"

That was what I wanted, to get her to laugh and see that awful moment at the monument for what it truly was—and to forget about the bottle I had thrown out the window.

"Good," I said. "Now you'll have to go to Florida with me. Who was it said you can't go home again?"

"But I'm not sure I like to be bossed."

"Who does?"

"Well, you've certainly taken charge this afternoon."

"Papa knows best," I said.

We flashed past the big rock but, going toward Old Hundred, you couldn't see the letters spelling "REPENT" unless you stopped.

"It was me or Wayne Bullock," I said. "Personally, I think you made the only possible choice."

She touched my knee. It was the most intimate gesture I had ever known her to make.

"I think so, too, Frank."

It was still hot, but, riding along in the Lincoln, we at least had a breeze. I was sorry to see the driveway to Old Hundred, to see our outing end. Just a glimpse of the white columns brought back too many things I hadn't even thought about while I had been absorbed with Ann.

We drove on back to the big graveled area in front of Harry's garage, where his visitors could always find plenty of parking space. There was shade under one of the big oaks that surrounded the house and I eased the Lincoln to a stop there.

"Well," I said. "Here we are."

"Yes. Back again."

I drummed my fingers on the steering wheel.

"Hell of a nice car."

"It's too big for me. I ought to get a little Ford or something, but I kind of like it."

"Sure. It's a terrific car."

"Frank?"

"Yes?"

"Will you kiss me?"

"I'll kiss you," I said, "but I'm not going to kiss anybody's goddamn family."

"I wouldn't ask you to."

Her body turned and she lay back between me and the steering wheel and her lips came up to meet mine. We kissed for a long time. There was still a faint odor of bourbon on her breath.

When I took my mouth away there were tears in her eyes but she was smiling.

"Have you had a lot of women?"

"What the hell kind of question is that?"

"I mean you're so *ex*pert."

"Ann," I said, "you ought not to say—"

"You don't care anything about who I am, do you? You just think of me as a woman."

I put my lips back on hers and she stirred against me. Things were beginning to get pretty close, even in that big car. It was a thin dress she was wearing and my hand was resting squarely on the zipper down its back. It took will power to push her away.

"That's right," I said. "I think of you as a woman, all right."

"It's so wonderful. It's so *wonderful* just to *be* something and not have to represent anything."

"Listen," I said. "It's broad open daylight. We'd better ..."

"I don't care. Suddenly I don't care about anything."

"Well, I do."

"Shut up." She laughed. "Did you see the way they looked when we drove by them there at the monument? Like I was a fallen woman or something."

"Yes," I said, "and you're damn well going to be, too, if you don't stop trying to press your ribs against my backbone."

"The hell with them all," she said. "The hell with the family. The hell with your modesty, too." Her soft lips pressed against mine again.

"Well," Maggie said, inches away from my ear, "if I ever saw a pair of lovers in need of a chaperon, you two are it."

I pushed Ann away and she sat up. Her skirt was far above her knees and I looked away while she twisted awkwardly, trying to get it down. Maggie watched, smiling.

"I suppose you volunteer your goddamned services," I said.

Maggie was still wearing the sun dress that exposed three quarters of her bountiful bosom. She leaned against the car door and I could smell the heavy perfume she always wore.

"I saw you drive in and wandered out to greet you," she said. "I never expected to walk into the middle of an orgy."

"Oh, for God's sake," I said. Maggie was one of those women who always tried to get her dancing partner to take her out to the dark end of the terrace at the Country Club. I think she held it against me because I had always refused.

"Really," Ann said. She was combing her hair and looking embarrassed but those decisive little lines appeared on her face again. "You might have coughed or kicked an old tin can or something."

"Well, Frank's been mooning around so much about Dolly, how was I to know he'd start necking with the first girl he got his hands on?"

I pushed open the car door and got out. "That's enough of that. I mean it, Maggie." A sort of cold fury almost choked me. She had had no right to bring up Dolly. Dolly was dead. Why did they all keep bringing up the dead?

"I mean, after all," Maggie said. "It was only a year ago she killed herself, and here you are—"

"Dolly didn't kill herself. I told you that once, Maggie. I don't want to hear it from you again."

"Frank," Ann said. She was standing beside me, but I hadn't even noticed her get out of the car. She slipped her hand into mine. "Don't mind her. Why do you have to be so mean, Maggie? Why do you have to interfere in everybody's life?"

"That isn't true," Maggie said. "Take you, for instance. I've never said a word to you about the way you drink so much."

"But Dolly *didn't* kill herself! Frank's right. You just don't know about last night."

"Last night?"

"Somebody tried to kill Frank last night."

Maggie turned and leaned her back against the car. Her face grayed. I watched it age ten years. Suddenly the big breasts no longer thrust up out of her girlish dress. They became pendulous and ugly, as if she had borne too many children and too many sorrows.

"You didn't know that, did you? There *are* a few things you don't know, Maggie ... like someone trying to drown Frank right out there in the swimming pool."

"No," Maggie whispered. "You're teasing, aren't you? Aren't you just saying that to—"

"It's true," I said. "Too bad he missed, eh?"

"Are you *sure?*" Maggie's eyes, blurred with tears, begged me to take back what had been said. "Are you *sure* it wasn't an accident?"

"No accident," I said.

Maggie flung herself away from the car. Her strong, insistent hands grabbed my arm, shook it.

"Then make Walter tell you! *Make* him, Frank!"

"Tell me what?"

"Whatever it is, whatever he won't talk about to me. *Make* him tell you before—"

"Cut it out," I said. "Let go of me."

She moved away, ungracefully. Looking at her bare arms and shoulders, I could see goose bumps breaking constantly on her skin. She was terrified; she was no more the old confident, bossy, prying Maggie than I was the old Frank she had intimidated so easily.

"You people," I said. "You run things your own way and then when something goes wrong you want someone to bail you out. You never think of the other guy, do you?"

"Frank," Ann said.

"They make me sick."

"But please make him tell you whatever he's hiding," Maggie said. Some of her dignity was coming back and I was glad to see it; I liked her better the old way, despite everything. She turned and ran, not looking back.

"Positively sick to my stomach," I said.

"Don't mind her," Ann said. "You've got to find out from Walter what the trouble is."

"Yes." I let go of her hand. "I'll go find him."

"Tell me about it, Frank. After you find him, come tell me about it."

"All right," I said. "All right, I will."

I turned and went across the gravel. When I looked back, she was still standing by the Lincoln. She waved and I waved back. She was an odd girl. I was not quite sure what I had uncovered in her, but it made me feel better to know she would be waiting.

CHAPTER TEN

WALKED in the general direction of the swimming pool. Long triangles of shade from the two giant oaks on the lawn sprawled toward me. I decided to get one of the deck chairs from the pool and bring it back under the trees. There I could think things over before I tackled Walter.

I came around the corner of the shrubbery and saw the green water of the pool still and empty. That was fine; I was in no mood to talk to anybody. My bones still ached and my head was beginning to pound again and I was uncomfortably aware of a cut on the inside of my right cheek.

Then I saw George. He was in his bathing suit and he was stretched out on a blanket on the flagstones by the pool. He was propped up on his elbows, looking down at Peggy, who was lying on her back, almost beneath him. She was in a bathing suit, too. They were all the way across the pool from me, but I saw her head strain up to meet his. His arms swept around her and they clung together, his big body covering hers. Her legs stretched out rigidly and then drew up in a sort of luxurious lethargy.

I moved cautiously away, down to one of the big trees, without my deck chair. I sat down with my back to the tree, my aching head against its rough bark, and stretched my legs out in front of me.

Pretty soon, George and Peggy came around the corner of the house and went across the porch. As he held the big screen door for his wife, I saw him give her a playful pat on her fanny. Her intimate little laugh came clearly down across the grass to me. I had heard Dolly laugh like that. I thought about Dolly a little bit.

When Walter came out, he was carrying a small gray bag and one golf club. He wore a golf cap and there was a pipe between his teeth. He surveyed the lawn, waved with the club to me, and went toward the level ground near the tennis court.

There was no use putting it off, so I got up and went after him. My body was aching and tired but I stepped out in long brisk strides. The sun was low in the late-afternoon sky, but it was still hot; its rays flared up off the green grass into my tired eyes.

Walter had emptied a dozen or more golf balls from the little bag and was addressing one of them. Walter was low-handicap man at the Club. He had tried to teach me but I had never found the patience for the game, or the money.

Walter swung as I came up to him. It looked like a nine iron he was using, and he went in deep and got some of Harry's grass and lofted the ball nicely toward the white meadow fence. It dropped with a lot of backspin and barely rolled beyond the lower rail.

"Not bad," I said. "Pretty soon you won't need a handicap at all."

He looked around and grinned, not at all surprised to see me.

"News for you. They took it away from me last summer."

"Maggie says you have more news than that."

The grin never wavered on his mouth, but it went abruptly dead in his eyes.

"What made her say a thing like that?" He pushed another ball into position and addressed it with the nine iron.

"You want to knock that off a minute?" I said. "I'm trying to talk to you, Walter."

He stroked smoothly into the ball, catching some more of Harry's grass. This time he had too much backspin and the ball rolled dead just short of the fence.

"I haven't got a single-track mind exactly," he said. "I'm listening." He nudged another ball out in front of him. His pipe bobbed in his mouth. "What kind of news did she say I had?"

"About who killed Dolly."

He stopped in the middle of his backswing and the club wavered slowly down.

"Did somebody kill Dolly?"

"Oh, yes," I said. "The same guy who tried to kill me last night. Was it you?"

He put the head of the golf club on the ground and leaned on the shaft, as if it were a walking cane. He took the pipe out of his mouth, carefully and slowly, looking at me all the time with eyes that were not so much shocked, not so much disbelieving, as cautious and—it almost seemed—disappointed.

"Somebody tried to kill you." It was a flat, unquestioning statement.

I nodded. He looked past me to the meadow and shook his head. It was a disapproving gesture but there was no surprise, no indignation in it.

"No, Frank, it wasn't me. Did you really think it was?"

I shrugged. I was in no mood to be careful of anybody's feelings. I told him what had happened, how I had not had a good enough look at my assailant even to know how tall he was, or if he was lean or stout.

"Maggie got right excited when I told her about it. She said I'd better make you tell me something. She didn't seem to know exactly what. She just seemed damn sure there was something."

He stopped leaning on the golf club.

"Maybe she's right, Frank. Maybe I can tell you … something."

"No time like the present."

"Maybe it's nothing. Maybe you'll think so."

"Maybe I won't."

"I was on emergency duty for the County Medical Society all that week when Dolly was killed. The Sheriff called me out as soon as they found the car. I can remember that morning as if it was yesterday. It was gray and ugly and the phone ringing is always a horrible sound just before the sun comes up. I knew somebody was dying when I heard it. It always rings that way when somebody's dying.

"When I got there, she was dead. The Sheriff knew it. He had already roped everything off and gone to notify Harry and Ellen. You could just look in the window of the car and see she was dead. They had sent for acetylene torches to get what was left of her out."

"That's not news," I said.

Walter's golf cap was one of those big funny ones with about twenty colors in it, the kind men in their thirties and forties wouldn't be caught dead on the golf course or at football games without; under it, his face had become round and bland and innocent again, and his eyes peered at me with what might have been either good humor or good-natured contempt.

"Dolly was a funny girl. You didn't know her except as a grown woman, Frank. I sort of wish you had known her when she was younger. I wish she could have been around you a long time sooner than she was."

"You seem to be the only one that does."

He ignored the sarcasm.

"She didn't marry you just because of your big blue eyes, you know. She was kind of funny, like I said, but she had reasons for what she did. She always had reasons."

"She was looking for something, Walter. A little while ago I was ready to believe it was death."

Walter waved a sweeping arm toward Old Hundred.

"Did you ever think what it would be to be brought up in a place like this, Frank? I don't mean just all the money. A lot of people have money. I mean to be brought up with that kind of blood running in you and a place like this holding memories over you every moment and traditions falling out of every closet you open. Did you ever think about that?"

"I thought about it, but I was brought up in a mill village with lint in my hair and patches on my britches. I wouldn't know anything about what it was like."

He wasn't listening. He pointed toward the house.

"Look at that. Right out of *Gone with the Wind.* And old Josephus preaching at her every day about the family and the traditions and showing her the old silver and the old linens and his grandmother's wedding dress and the old rose pressed in the family Bible. That and her own mother scared of her shadow, scared she'd displease the old man, and acting as if he was God, as if all his people were gods, and teaching Dolly to think the same way. Imagine all that and—"

"All right," I said. "I've already spent years imagining it. Let's don't go over it any more, if you don't mind."

"Well, I said Dolly was funny. I think all that had a lot to do with it. I think she grew up looking for a world that doesn't exist any more. Probably never did. And when she got old enough to realize it, it was too late. She never had a chance to learn to love any other kind of world. What she had to try to do was to get along in a world that wasn't hers, that maybe never had any room for a girl like her. Do you follow me, Frank?"

"I'd have to think about that some," I said. "I never looked at it just that way."

"Well, maybe that's what Maggie meant." He winked at me. "Maybe she just meant I could give you a new slant on things."

"The hell she did."

He shrugged, grinning faintly. I ought to knock that silly grin right off your teeth, I thought.

"Frank, I could be wrong. Not in what I saw, but in what I made of it. People don't always make the same things out of the same facts."

"Will you for God's sake say it and get it over with?"

He grinned again and the muscles of my arms bunched and flexed. In another second I would have hit him right in the middle of that grin.

"When I examined the body, it was so battered that any number of things or combination of them could actually have caused death. But right about here"—he touched the back of his head—"there was a big cut and bruise. Something had hit her hard there and fractured her skull. Maybe killed her, but there's no way to be sure about that now."

I closed my eyes. "Somebody had hit her there?"

"I didn't say that. But I tried hard to figure it out at the time and I can't for the life of me tell what it could have been, considering the position of the body and the way the wreck happened."

"Then somebody hit her. That's what you think, isn't it, Walter?"

He shook his head, smiling again. "What I think is immaterial. It's what you think that's going to be important. Because neither of us can prove a thing."

"Don't try to dodge it. Don't give me any of that goddamn cracker-barrel philosophy of yours, either."

He laughed out loud.

"Matter of fact, Frank, I made that examination in a hell of a hurry. There was a tremendous amount of blood and a lot of people pushing around and all. I could be wrong, you know."

In the shimmering afternoon heat my head began to grow light. Far beyond me the horizon began to move across my vision like a cyclorama.

"You aren't wrong," I said. "Somebody hit her. Somebody killed her. I knew it all along and now I'm sure."

"Of course you're sure," Walter said. "You can't prove it but you're sure. You would be."

"What did you tell me any of this for if you aim to back out now?"

He put the pipe back in his mouth. It made him look quite wise and almost good-natured.

"What makes you think I haven't told you everything you need to know, Frank?"

The horizon was moving faster past my eyes and I had to shut them to stop it. When I opened them, I noticed how low the sun was; but its shimmer was white, as if a whole host of photographers' flash bulbs had been exploded at the same moment and kept at their peak.

"Thanks," I said. "Thanks a million, Walter."

He addressed his golf ball again; he did not look at me as he spoke.

"I don't know what you aim to do with what I've told you, but I won't tell it to anybody else. Especially in a court. I wouldn't even remember talking to you if it ever came to that."

His backswing was a little jerky but he caught just the right amount of grass with the clubhead and the ball's arc was graceful as the weightless lilt of a sparrow. It rolled dead directly under the lowest rail of the fence.

"You figure it all out," he said. "Then get the hell away from here, Frank. Get away and stay away."

I went back and sat under my tree again. There didn't seem to be much else to do and it was shady and cool against the great trunk.

I began to take out and examine each word Walter had said, as if it were a secret jewel, as if all of them were a fortune in rare, hidden stones. Walter had said it was all there, that all I had to do was to figure it out and then go away.

Ellen came out of the house and walked across the lawn toward me. The sun was going down behind her and through her thin skirt I could see the shaded outlines of her long fine legs.

She walked up so close to me that, looking up, I saw her out of perspective; she seemed much taller and her face seemed much longer and narrower and, in the gathering darkness, less perfectly proportioned.

"Maggie told me," she said. "I won't have that kind of wild talk, Frank. I've had entirely too much from you already."

"What wild talk?"

"About somebody pushing you into the pool. You know nobody pushed you into the pool. You fell in or something if you were in it at all and you know it and I am *not* going to have you spreading anything else around just because you've been ... sick."

"Are you threatening me, Ellen?"

She leaned forward, her hands going to her hips.

"Call it what you want. Think what you want. But I can't have you carrying tales like that about Old Hundred."

I nodded. It seemed to me that she was leaning still farther over, that her head was growing larger but more indistinct in the gloom. I could reach up and touch her breasts. The thought made me shiver.

"Not even if the tales are true," I said. "Not even if you have to try to send me back where I came from to shut me up."

"I told you. Think what you want to."

She really was leaning farther over. I had the absurd notion of reaching up and grabbing her and jerking her down to the ground, of beating her face against the earth.

"Do you understand me, Frank?"

"Go away," I said. My tongue was thick as old biscuit dough.

Her stare was as icily contemptuous as a cat's. "Just so you understand," she said.

She walked back to the house. I watched her all the way. It seemed impossible that I had ever wanted her, even subconsciously. It seemed impossible that anyone should ever have wanted that chill, that precision. But I had wanted her and, watching her, I thanked God that that was over, that she could no longer dominate me.

Yet... Ellen lived in a world of arrogance; no other is so insecure, can survive so little. I felt strangely sorry for her as she reached the porch of her big white castle, around which she could build no moat. In a way, she and I were alike; we had more in common than either of us had ever admitted.

It was a strange time and a strange place to think of Christmas, but without warning I was immersed in one of those clouds of reminiscence that sometimes comes into a perfectly clear sky. For a moment, memory struggled furiously at the edge of my mind; then it triumphed, just as she disappeared into Old Hundred, just as the slap of the screen door came like a signal across the darkening lawn.

"All right," Harry said, "we'll draw straws to see who plays Santa Claus."

"But you're always Santa Claus," Ellen said.

She put a small white angel figurine under the tree with a determined little slap.

"I know, but I thought since Frank's here we could—"

"Never mind about me," I said. "You don't have to worry about me, Harry."

"It's custom, Harry. The head of the house is always Santa Claus."

Ellen rose smoothly to her feet. She had been sitting almost under the huge green tree that rose to the ceiling of Old Hundred's main room. "Isn't that right, Dolly?"

"Let's open the presents now," Dolly said. "I can't wait till Frank sees what I got him."

"But we *never* open them till Christmas morning. And Harry is always Santa Claus. I don't see why we have to change just because—"

"I don't either," I said, too loudly. "Harry, you be Santa Claus."

"Well, I want to open my presents now." I could see that Dolly was teasing Ellen. She gave me a secret little wink and I knew she was pleased with me about Santa Claus. We had been married over a year and I had learned to read her like a book.

Harry went over to her and shoveled a handful of popcorn into her mouth.

"Maybe that'll hold you till morning. You're worse than a child."

She bit his hand when she took the popcorn in her mouth and he jumped away, wringing it as if a rattler had struck it, being very comical. Everybody was being very comical except Ellen, who kept saying we'd never finish the tree if we didn't hurry.

Christmas at Old Hundred was a quiet time. It was the one holiday Harry and Ellen refused to observe with parties and merrymaking. But they usually followed it with a huge New Year affair and few of their insistent acquaintances complained too much.

Harry and Ellen were inclined to such Christmas activities as making chains out of popcorn, hand-drawing their greeting cards, and making their own decorations. Once they even roasted apples but found they didn't like them that way and went back to eating them raw.

I was so glad to be there that I would have been happy to eat a roasted apple. The day before I had come home to the great drafty apartment on Sycamore Street and found Dolly gone. I did not need a note—even if she had left one—to tell me where she was. The apartment had a sly air of desertion. It had that same atmosphere every time she went to Old Hundred.

There was no way to tell how long she would be gone—an hour, a day, a month. I stood looking about the empty living room, at the dainty litter she had fled from—a stocking by the magazine rack, a tiny belt over the back of a chair, a kerchief dangling across the end table, one glove on the telephone table, its mate on the floor—and I told myself that this time, when she came back, I wouldn't be waiting. This time

I wouldn't even wait to hurl vain foolish questions into the great gloomy magnificence of the symphonies, into the white misery of her tight unanswering face; this time was too much, even for me.

I went into the kitchen and got a half-full bottle of whisky from the cabinet above the sink and a water glass from the cabinet above the drainboard and took them both back into the living room. I sat down on the sofa by the fireplace and began to get drunk. I managed this in no time at all and went to sleep on the sofa with the empty bottle lying mockingly on my chest.

I had awakened that morning—Christmas Eve—with a vicious throbbing hangover. I conquered that with a hard day's work at tasks that could easily have been done after the holidays, but that took my mind not only off my livid eyes and pounding head, but also off Dolly.

I walked home that night through streets ringing with amplified Christmas carols, among crowds laden with brilliant packages and beaming amiably in that fatuous mood of generosity and gaiety and conviviality and secret acquisitiveness that merchants and ministers like to call "the Christmas spirit." The garish wreaths and lights and figurines hanging above me in the streets were as unreal as midnight dreams and I clamped my jaws and hurried rudely along, ignoring even those townspeople so inflamed with the holiday mood as to offer me the season's greetings, if not their own.

I went up the cold dark stairway, smelling the burned odor of the cookies Mrs. Barnes had baked indefatigably for weeks and, presumably, eaten by herself. By God, I thought, I can't get out of here quick enough. Not nearly quick enough.

But there was a note from Dolly pinned to the back of the sofa. Characteristically, it was written in her barely legible scrawl on a torn piece of gift-wrapping paper, although there was plenty of stationery in the apartment:

Darling—

I've been horrible again. I don't blame you if you don't forgive me but Harry says come to Old Hundred for Christmas. Do, please, if you love your crazy

DOLLY

Did you drink all that whisky?

I crumpled the note in my hand. The muscles of my face were aching. Suddenly I was grinning as fatuously as the downtown mobs. I was grinning and mumbling and I wadded the note up and threw it into the fireplace and hurried into the bedroom to change. My chest was bursting, my throat was bursting, my whole body was bursting with the glad swift bound of blood through my veins. I was going to Dolly, I would go to her no matter what she did, no matter how she hurt me. I would always go to her if I were able, and, knowing that, discovering it in that hurried scrawl on that torn gaudy paper, I knew too that I had made some deep choice, some irrevocable decision that I would never have to face again.

In a few minutes now, it would actually be Christmas Day. There had been—after one short glance had passed between Dolly and me and made everything right, offered her silent apology and my glad acceptance—a big dinner and a fruitcake rich with brandy and lots more brandy during the rest of the evening. Things had been gay; even I had had a good time watching Dolly and Harry carry on like a couple of kids. They had been so noisy and playful that it was almost possible for me to forget the faintly reproachful presence of Ellen.

"That finishes the tree," she said. "Turn off the lights, Harry."

The tree was covered with small decorations that, over the years, the Thompson family and then Harry and Ellen had made themselves. There were paper cutouts and wood carvings and delicate loops of beads and plaster figures. Under the tree there was a Nativity scene carved this year by Ellen from some plastic material. The tree itself had been cut from Old Hundred timber and only its lights had been bought.

Harry turned the room lights out and the tree lights on at the same time. The tree was colorful and mistily beautiful, sending a dim happy glow out into the big quiet room.

"Oh, it's beautiful," Dolly said. "It's always so beautiful at Old Hundred at Christmas."

"That's the prettiest tree we ever had," Harry said. "Isn't that gorgeous, Ellen?"

"I never saw anything like it," I said.

"It's a little gaudy," Ellen said. "Too many lights."

"*Don't* take any off," Dolly said. "It's so beautiful."

"Right over there on the left. Harry, don't you think I'd better take a string off right over there?"

"Where? By the antique Madonna?"

"I never saw anything like it," I said. At home, we had always had a small tree bought from the grocery store and decorated with one string of dime-store lights, some tinsel, and a ratty string or two of red-paper chain.

"Well, I think I'll take a string off. It's so gaudy. It's not traditional."

"But you're wrong," Dolly cried. "You'll spoil it if you touch it one more time."

Ellen was already moving toward the tree. Harry caught her hand.

"If Dolly likes it, let it stay. This is sort of a homecoming, isn't it?"

"A what?" Ellen said. "For who?"

"A home-coming for Dolly. That sort of makes it her tree, doesn't it?"

Dolly threw her arms around his neck.

"You sweet old ham, you!"

"I didn't know she'd been anywhere," Ellen said. But she moved away from the free.

"Here," Harry said. He pushed Dolly way. "Whoa there a minute, girl. We're forgetting the most important thing."

I didn't know what it could be. I thought they had everything. Brandy was warm and exciting in my stomach. This was the way to live, I thought. This was the way to do things, even Christmas. Money wasn't everything and neither was family, but if you had them both you could certainly manage well without whatever was left.

Harry hurried out of the room. Ellen busied herself picking up some stray papers and ribbon that had fallen around the tree. Dolly came over to me.

"You're having a good time, aren't you, Frank?"

I waved my brandy glass.

"Merry Christmas," I said. "Wassail and all that."

"You *are*, I know you are."

I sipped the brandy. "God rest ye merry, gentlemen," I said.

She pinched my wrist. "I'll God-rest-you if you don't start taking part in things. Harry asked us especially because—"

"Right," I said. "I perceive precisely what you mean." The radio had been playing Christmas music all evening. There was a Crosby pop number playing now. I handed my brandy glass to Dolly. "Silent night," I said. "Holy night. God bless us every one."

I went over to Ellen. She was still looking over the tree.

"Reminds me of Rockefeller Center," I said. "Only with antique Madonnas."

In the dim glow of the tree, I could see a sharp look pinch in around her eyes.

"You should know, Frank. You're an … electrician."

I bowed. "Sometimes I even shock myself," I said. "Might I have this dance, madam?"

Harry came in again, still hurrying.

"Look what we almost forgot, Ellen." He was holding the ugly old china dog they had won at some long-ago county fair. "We always put it under the tree," he said. "I never did know why, but we always do."

Ellen almost snatched it from his hands.

"I wasn't forgetting it. I was going to put it where I always do." She knelt and put the dog near the Nativity scene, running her hand along its smooth china back, its long pointed tail.

I wondered again what secret, profound meaning that cheap prize had for Harry and Ellen. Perhaps its very cheapness made it valuable to them. Perhaps they didn't own anything else cheap.

"Is its name Leander?" I said. But no one heard me.

Ellen stood up and turned to me. "I'd love to dance."

She moved into my arms and we glided off, whirling out into the center of the room. She was the best dancer I had ever held in my arms, but there was no pleasure in it. It was too expert, too drilled. I twisted her roughly around, trying to find the living woman beyond that metronomic precision. She was pliable as cloth in my hands.

"You're very strong, aren't you?" she said.

Over her shoulder, I saw Harry and Dolly dancing too.

"Very. I could break you in half."

She smiled. "Would you like to?"

"Sometimes."

She smiled again, shrugging. "At least you're honest. No wonder Dolly liked you."

Dolly and Harry were dancing very closely. They had always danced well together. They had gone to dancing school and, so Dolly had told me, they had always been made to get up and demonstrate for the other kids. It had given her and Harry a sort of feeling about their dancing, Dolly said.

"How do you mean, no wonder?"

"That type of woman always likes your type. Or thinks she does."

I stopped dancing, holding her away from me.

"What the hell do you mean, that type of woman?"

"The kind that likes to be … looked after."

"I don't like cracks about Dolly."

"I wasn't making any cracks about her."

"All right," I said. "That's just one thing I don't like, that's all."

She came back into my arms. She was so light, moved so effortlessly, I hardly knew we were dancing again. It had become very warm in the room. Her body touching mine made things even warmer. The brandy was a generous glow in my veins.

"I believe you're trying," Ellen said.

"Trying what?"

"To break me in two."

I had not realized how closely I was holding her. Now, at the words, I became aware of her breasts against me, of her arched back and her face peering up into mine, faintly amused.

Crosby's voice broke off abruptly. The radio went dead and then there was an announcer shouting madly and the sound of cheering from somewhere—perhaps a city night club—and over that you could hear a jangly orchestra blaring out "Jingle Bells."

"It's Christmas," Ellen said. She sounded as if she could take it or leave it alone. She pulled a little away from me.

"Merry Christmas!" I heard Dolly call. I swung Ellen around just as Harry shouted:

"Christmas gift, everybody!"

He waved at us, then put his arms around Dolly and pulled her close. He bent his head and they kissed, just as if it were New Year's Day instead of Christmas.

The brandy had made me lose caution. I grasped Ellen and pulled her close again. Her head went back and a startled look came into her eyes but she made no move to evade me.

Her lips were thin and heatless. I felt them stretch back across her teeth. A tremor went down her hard body, as if she found my mouth on hers revolting. A terrible hidden anger lit some unknown fuse in me. I clamped her body against mine and forced my tongue between those taut lips and those white perfect teeth and against the roof of her rigid mouth. I opened my eyes and looked down into hers.

She was not looking at me at all. Her eyes were open wide and I knew she had not closed them while I kissed her. She was looking past my shoulder. I took my mouth away from hers but she didn't move, not even to draw away from me.

My fingers dug deep into her flesh and I shook her a little, anger popping like static inside my head. I ground my mouth down on hers again. I kept my eyes open, kept them staring into hers. She didn't even know I was kissing her.

I lifted my head and looked where she was looking, at Harry and Dolly, and saw what she saw. As I watched, they began to dance again, laughing. I remembered the night of my birthday when I had come home and found the music playing and their two heads silhouetted against the firelight. It was the same now. There was some bond, some attachment—of blood, or tradition, of old lost childhood—between Harry and Dolly that nothing would ever disturb, ever destroy; and nobody would ever share it, either.

They laughed about something. They were dancing hard, trying to keep up with "Jingle Bells," and doing very well at it.

"They're good," I said. "Aren't they good together, Ellen?"

"Very." Her voice was dry and thin and stretched, the way her lips had been. It made me feel better, a whole lot better, to know she had seen it too, to know Ellen Thompson didn't have everything after all. Nobody had everything except Harry and Dolly.

"How does it feel to be on the outside?" I said. "How does it feel to be out here in left field with me?"

"You," she said, in that stretched voice like tissue paper crumpling, that voice which now for the first time had in it the raw sound of hurt. "You ... How long do you think she'll want you?" Then, a rising bursting edge of triumph in the words, as malicious as the sibilant gossip of idle old ladies: "Do you think you'll last any longer with her than anything else ever has?"

"Jingle Bells" ended and the announcer and the loud night-club cheering were cut off as if someone had throttled a thousand drunken men at once. Crosby came back, but this time he was singing *"Adeste Fideles."* I couldn't dance to that, even if I had wanted to, and I took my arms from around Ellen and walked away, over to where Dolly had put my brandy glass. I found it and went on to where Harry and Dolly stood looking at the Christmas tree. That affinity, that insistent bond between them was almost a reek in the steam-heated air of the room.

I held up the glass in a toast to Dolly. "Yes, Virginia," I said, "there *is* a Santa Claus." I drank the rest of the brandy in one gulp.

Harry and Dolly looked at me from four identical blank eyes. For a moment so long I felt shock burn and tingle in each separate nerve of my body, I knew they didn't recognize me, hardly even saw me. Then Dolly threw herself against me the way she did everything else, impulsively, generously, holding back nothing, her strong arms going hard around me, closing tight.

"Merry Christmas, Frank! Merry Christmas, darling!"

Over her small golden head, I looked into Harry's eyes. They were still blank, still unrecognizing, but while I watched they changed and knew me.

"Christmas gift!" he shouted. "Christmas gift, everybody!"

CHAPTER ELEVEN

B UT THIS was not Christmas. This was the Fourth of July, years later. This was now.

The day wore on and the sun in its long inevitable arc sank to the horizon. Lights began to come on one by one in the windows of Old Hundred, reflecting like mirrors the people they illuminated—bright and brazen in Maggie's room and mellow and glowing in Harry's and with a tentative hopefulness I found heartbreaking in Ann's. They didn't come on at all in my room and that seemed as appropriate as it was logical.

Something was going around my head in a huge circle, like a June bug I had twirled at the end of a string when I was a child. It was not getting any nearer but it was not getting any farther away, either. Finally I stood up and brushed the grass blades from my trousers. It was almost completely dark. I had not eaten all day; my stomach felt drawn and squeezed. Perhaps Ann and I could go somewhere for dinner, somewhere away from these people and this place.

I put my hands in my pockets and started toward the house. The long smooth stone was still in my pocket. I had had it in my hand off and on all day and I wondered why I had kept it. I pulled it out and in the fading light looked at it more closely. In my pocket the grit had been brushed away so that it gleamed as if it had been polished. One end of it was jagged, the other pointed, almost sharp. It was smooth as china.

The lights had come on triumphantly in George's room. Now I saw Peggy's silhouette pass before the window, pulling a blouse or slip or something over her head. She and George had made an afternoon of it.

Maybe George was better off than any of us, I thought. What difference did it make if Peggy had married beneath herself for his money, if she had spent all her time since then trying to regain the prestige she had lost? What difference did it make that the only way she could do this, in Huntsville, was to please Ellen Thompson at any price—up to and including the self-respect of George Johnson?

What difference did any of that make when the two of them had what I had seen at the pool? None of us knew what compulsions George understood in Peggy, what singular need she filled for him. In her, in him, in everyone, the stuffs of life had struck their own peculiar balance, for which there could be no accounting.

The hell with it, I thought. I tossed the long white stone into the gathering darkness and went on toward the house. The June bug was still whirling around my head but I tried to ignore it.

Then I thought of Harry and Dolly. My theory of compulsions and needs wouldn't work with them. They had had everything. They had always had everything.

The June bug went away. I stopped. My heart began a great irregular pounding. In the still summer evening gloom, I could almost hear it.

In front of me the great white house rose against a sky from which all but the last orange rays had faded; an early moon had already risen and looked whitely down at me. Ideas leaped swiftly into my brain. They grew out of next to nothing. They were so repellent, so fantastic, I pushed them immediately away. But they came back, uglier than ever, making me nearly sick to my stomach.

I went a few steps across the grass, got down on my knees, and began to feel around where I had thrown it. My hands fumbled frantically in front of me. I scuffed about on my knees in an ever-widening circle. It had to be about where I was looking because I hadn't thrown it very hard. Or had I had it in my right hand? Had I thrown it the other way? Perhaps I wasn't even near the right spot. Perhaps...

"Hey," George said. "You looking for something?"

His big knees were right in front of my face. I reared back on my haunches like a spooky horse and looked up the length of his legs and trunk to his massive head, far above me. There was just enough light left to make out its outline against the purple sky. It reminded me of that dark figure by the pool the night before.

"I saw you fumbling around from the porch. I got some matches here."

He was holding out a book of paper matches and I took them in a shaky hand. I could feel the irregular pound and flow of blood all through me.

"Thanks, George."

"Hell, I'll help you look. What did you lose?"

I struck a match. In its yellow flare, I could see plainly that it was nowhere in front of me.

"Nothing much. Just a little white thing. Sort of a keepsake."

He nodded and squatted ponderously. "Sentimental value, eh?" He patted the grass experimentally. "I remember once Peg lost an earring and she said it wasn't much but it had sentimental value and I said yes and it cost twenty-five dollars, too."

I struck another match, hunting carefully.

"Is this it?" George said.

The match dropped out of my fingers to the grass. It flared brilliantly, then went out. I reached over and took it out of his hands.

"That's it."

"Funny kind of a rock, isn't it?"

"You'd be surprised," I said. "You might not even believe it."

There was no light in Harry's den and I could see nothing but the vague shape of the desk and the lighter oblong of the window.

In the dark, the room had an air of disuse and emptiness I had never noticed before.

I went in and switched on the desk lamp. The light didn't help much. I pulled at a leather-bound edition of the works of Sidney Lanier; it stuck and when I got it out there was a clear outline where it had been on the shelf. I pulled out *The House of the Seven Gables* and *The Nigger of the Narcissus* and *Lyrics from Cottonland* and they left the same outlines. No one had taken books off those shelves for months. They hadn't even been dusted, except along their spines.

I took a record at random from the shelves above the player; the record jackets were dusty, too. The one I picked was a Schumann trio. I couldn't take chamber music then or any other time, so I put it back and searched until I found one of my favorites, Brahms' D-major symphony, with which Dolly had made me familiar. I turned the volume up as far as it would go and sat down to wait in the chair by the big globe.

Harry had spent a good deal of money for his record player and it had a lot of volume and a lot of bass. I expect you could hear it all over the house. Before long, the door opened and Harry looked around its edge. I turned the volume down.

"Are you deaf or practicing to be?" he said.

"I like them loud. Dolly used to play them that way."

"Not that loud, for God's sake." He came on into the room, looking curiously at me. "Did you have a good nap under the tree?"

I nodded and took the tone arm off the record and switched off the player. He went around the desk and sat down, still watching me. I put the Brahms carefully back in its jacket.

"Why, yes," I said. "I had a pretty good nap."

"Well, a man can go a long way and not find a place where he can relax like he can at Old Hundred. My father always said that."

I stood up and put the record back on the shelf, then eased down into the leather chair again.

"That's true," I said. "Things have been a little exciting this trip, but that's perfectly true, Harry."

"You want a drink? All the makings are in the cabinet behind you there."

I could just see old Josephus' portrait over Harry's head. He still glared down as if he disapproved of dens and people like me, but his stare didn't disturb me any more. I looked back at the portrait without interest. It was hard to remember why a bad picture of an unpleasant old man, dead for many years, had ever bothered me. There were no cotton futures in heaven and this old man would not have been so much without cotton futures. You could look at Peggy Johnson and be sure of that; nothing preserved tradition quite like money, lots of money.

"Harry, do you remember the night Dolly and I came back from Florida?"

He cleared his throat. The sound was startling in the quiet musty room. I let my eyes drift slowly from the portrait of old Josephus down to the white pool of light around the desk.

"I raised a little hell, didn't I?"

I nodded. "But that same night Dolly said to me, 'Frank, don't worry about Harry. He'll be for us in the long run. He'll be for anything I want.'"

He stared at me.

"Did she really say that, Frank?"

"Yes."

He shook his head. "She was a good kid. Dolly was ... she was a hell of a good kid."

"You loved her, didn't you? Even if she was only your half sister."

He reared back in his swivel chair and began to trace with his finger on the glass top of the desk the outline of a shadow from his pen set. There was no resemblance at all between him and the portrait over his head.

"I never thought of her as a half sister. She was a Thompson, too, just as much as I was. A hell of a lot more than that mother of hers ever was. You know, I can't get over her saying that about me. I was damned snotty that night."

I sat up in my chair and braced my forearm along the outer edge of his huge desk, just beyond the rim of light.

"I guess Dolly understood how things were," I said.

Peggy started playing "Begin the Beguine" on the piano in the living room. I knew it was her because of the violent swoops into the bass keys that she thought constituted a Latin feeling. Still, the music broke the quiet and it had rhythm and flow. I was glad to hear it.

"What does that mean?" Harry leaned farther back in his swivel chair.

"Well, you always were for her, weren't you? In the long run?"

"I suppose so."

"I've found out a few things since I talked to you at noon, Harry. About how Dolly died."

Peggy thundered mightily along on "Begin the Beguine." There was a sudden heavy thumping on the stairs, as if George might have been coming down them two at a time, bent on stopping her.

"I thought you had that foolishness out of your mind," Harry said. "You gave me to understand that you had."

I moved an impatient hand out into the center of his desk and let it point at him.

"That was before I found these things out. That was before I knew about the blow to the base of her skull." I pulled my hand back out of the light and touched the back of my head, leaning forward so he could see. "About here."

He was quiet a long time. Peggy finished "Begin the Beguine."

"You know what happened to her in that wreck, Frank. She could have…"

I shook my head slowly and he stopped. My hand fell across the desk again, pointing at his stomach.

"Somebody hit her with something." I put my hand back on my head. "Right there."

"Who told you that?" His voice rapped suddenly at me like a prosecutor's, sharp, staccato.

"I always thought you and Dolly had everything, Harry. But I forgot the one thing you didn't have."

"Frank, I want to know where you heard that nonsense about somebody hitting her."

I heard the light slap of the screen door that opened onto the front porch. The sounds of his breathing and mine were plain in the dim still room with its faint musty odor and its vague air of emptiness and uselessness.

"I forgot you didn't have each other."

I stood up and reached into my pocket and tossed the tail of the china dog on the glass top of the desk. It made a dull clink, like a chain rattling.

"And what I want to know," I said, "is what really happened to that china dog you and Ellen were so proud of."

As if my words had been a cue, Peggy started playing "Summertime." For a moment I thought Harry hadn't heard me, hadn't seen what lay on his desk. Hope and fear mixed in me. Couldn't he see what I was talking about? Didn't he know what I meant?

"Frank...leave it alone. Leave it alone for her sake." His whisper was agonized and imploring.

I reached across the desk and bunched the front of his white shirt in my hand and pulled him to his feet.

"It's a dirty word, isn't it, Harry? It's a dirty, filthy word you'd like to keep anybody from saying, isn't it?"

Peggy's music was suddenly loud and clear. Harry's face went gray. Its flesh sagged in great bloated patches from its bones. His hands came up, clutching my arms, shaking them feebly, as if I were a nightmare that could be driven away.

I hated him with pure perfect violent energy and I struck him open-handed across his twisted mouth. Blood showed tinily in its left corner.

"Incest," I said. "That's the word you don't want me to say, isn't it?"

I began to shake him.

"And here's another one. Murder. You like that any better, Harry?"

I thrust him away from me as hard as I could and he went down into the desk chair. Its swivel shrieked and he went over backward, his feet describing a flailing arc up in front of my face. He struck the floor with a startling thump.

"You killed her," I said. "You took her and ruined her and then you killed her."

I moved around the desk to where I could look down at him. He lay huddled, his face hidden from me. Then muscles began to bunch in his shoulders and he pushed himself up with his arms.

"And don't give me that for-her-sake crap, either. You killed her because you were scared somebody would find out about you." He slumped back to the floor. "Because you were too much of a coward to face the truth about yourself."

"All right, Frank," Ellen said behind me. "Now you go over there and sit down and be quiet."

She was standing just inside the door. Her face was calm, although its flesh was drawn tight over her nose and cheeks. In the dim light I could not see her well until she took a step forward. There were two spots of color high on her cheeks and she held a small automatic pistol in her hand.

I backed slowly around the desk, watching her, and felt behind me for the leather armchair. It squished softly when I settled down into it.

"I didn't think you were sane," Ellen said. "I didn't think you were in your right mind from the minute you came back."

She reached behind her and closed the door. Peggy's music died away sharply. I could hear Harry shuffling and struggling on the floor. It took him a long time to get to his feet.

Ellen turned halfway around, still holding the gun on me, and locked the door. Then she came calmly across the room and sat down on the sofa, tucking her skirt demurely under her knees. She was wearing a sheer white dress gathered with pastel ribbon at the neck. The dress made her look much younger than she was, like a high-school girl; it made the gun, blackly outlined against it, doubly evil, doubly fascinating.

"Ellen?" Harry's voice squeaked like his swivel chair. "What are you going to do?"

His face was still gray, but color was beginning to drift down from his temples and his flesh looked firm again, as if he had been kneading it back into place with his fingers.

Ellen's voice was crisp, efficient.

"He's crazy, isn't he? Didn't he attack you?"

My stomach began to quiver. Harry righted the swivel chair and sagged into it. I risked another look and met his staring eyes. They blinked blearily, cleared, focused, bleared again.

"Frank, I never ..." He swallowed hard. "I never wanted this."

"No. You only wanted Dolly, didn't you? You only wanted your own sister. That was all you wanted."

"Half sister," Ellen said. "She wasn't his real sister."

"All right, *half* sister, then. Does that makes it half incest if she was only his half sister?"

Her body went rigid and the gun leaped forward, pointing directly at my chest.

"I want you to be quiet," she said. "I don't want you to say another word."

It was incongruous. I could hardly believe that here in Harry's den at the hands of two people I had known for years, whom I had so often envied and emulated, I was going to meet death at last; not with Peggy's showy music in the house, not with the echoes of George's great clumping footfalls on the stairs still in my ears, not with the crickets and bullfrogs of Old Hundred making their noises outside the window, not with old Josephus staring down with his enduring gruff disapproval. I looked up at him and wild laughter raced into my chest. It never came out.

"I'll tell you how it was," Ellen said. "Just how it was with him and your precious Dolly. You don't have to guess."

I could see she had for once a great human urge to explain herself; she had to reassert her own assurance. She was not talking to Harry or even, really, to me.

"I tried not to believe it. Then when I had to believe it, I tried to ignore it. For a long time I tried to ignore it. But … that night I came down to get a book. And there they were. The music was going so loud they couldn't hear me and there they were on this sofa right where I'm sitting." She touched it with her free hand. "They didn't even see me for three minutes. For three whole minutes I stood there in the door and listened to the music and watched him kissing her and feeling her and opening her clothes and listened to the—"

"All right," I said, squeezing my eyes shut against the pain of the image her words conjured. "Stop it, Ellen."

"At first I thought she was struggling to get away from him and I started to … I wanted to kill him, I wanted to tear him to pieces. Then I saw her hands on him and I saw what it really was."

"Goddamn it, will you stop it, Ellen?"

"It kept going through my head like the music that that was Harry, that was my husband doing those vile things, and that if they ever found out, if anybody ever … knew … It kept going through my head what it would be like if they knew and if every time I walked down the street they pointed. I could see those fingers pointing at me all the time."

"It was all a bad dream," Harry said, his voice moving in on hers smoothly and on cue, so that while her words floated away toward the high old ceiling, his own took up the thread and began to ravel it out to its sordid end. "It was all like a bad dream and every morning now I wake up thinking about it and thanking God it wasn't real. But then I have to remember it was real. Oh, God, I think, it was real, and all the rest of it comes piling in on top … all of it from way back when we were children and both of us hated her mother. We would pretend to be married the way we thought they ought to be and—"

"Harry," Ellen said. "That's enough." But he paid no attention to her.

"We never wanted it that way. We tried—my God, how we both tried—but it seemed like something would always happen and without wanting to or meaning to it would start all over."

His voice went up an octave and became almost shrill. "And my dear wife … We hadn't been married a year before she had to have a separate room, so she could be pure and unsullied and unpregnant. That helped a lot."

"Harry," Ellen said again. This time her clear voice dominated his and he quit talking.

In the lamplight I could see his hands twisting together on the glass top of the desk, making the brittle dry sound of old leaves being raked from the lawn. I was no longer angry at him or repelled by him or even shocked; I simply felt nothing for him at all.

"I'm not blind," Ellen said. "That was when I started trying to ignore it. And what does any of that matter, anyway? It's what you did that matters."

His entwined hands lifted and fell back hard on the glass.

"But it was something we *couldn't* … Listen. That night I was almost asleep on the sofa and it was late and I was just lying there listening to the music. Dolly came in. I didn't think anything, it had been a long time and we thought it was all over. But she lit a cigarette and came over and put one in my mouth and bent down to light it. I don't know ... all of a sudden nothing mattered but Dolly, nothing but her and ..." He shook his head. His hands parted and slipped off the tabletop.

"Then the music ended," Ellen said. "The same thing started all over again. I knew I wasn't going to be able to ignore this and I felt something move. It was whatever makes your legs go and I walked across the room and picked up the first thing I laid my hands on. Harry saw me and pushed her away and called something to me. She began to turn her head but I hit her before she could even see who it was. She didn't make any noise. And do you know what he did?"

There was rising glee in her voice and I braced back against the leather of the chair, seeing in the quick gush of emotion the moment when she would pull the trigger. Instead, her whole body relaxed and for the first time the barrel of the pistol dipped and I couldn't see the evil ring of its muzzle.

"He let her fall on the floor. He let her roll right off the sofa on the floor."

CHAPTER TWELVE

GATHERED MY LEGS under me to leap for the pistol, but it came back up and pointed steadily at my chest.

"But how did you know?" Ellen said. "And does anybody else?"

I nodded at the tail of the china dog, which still lay on Harry's desk.

"I found that out at the rock where the wreck was. It took me a long time to connect it with anything. It didn't have to be what I finally decided it was, but when I tossed it down there on the desk and saw the way Harry acted, I knew I was right, that what she'd been hit with was your china dog."

Ellen nodded. "The tail must have got caught in her clothes when it broke over her head. Think of it lying there all this time. A whole year. I swept up all the rest of the pieces."

"That was goddamned neat of you," I said.

"And then last night, in your room, I saw that piece lying there on your dresser. I knew what it was right away. I didn't know what it meant, but I knew it meant something that you had it."

"Then it was you ..."

"Why did you have to learn to swim, Frank? It would have been so much simpler that way."

The calm words made me afraid at last. I had always known she was cold-blooded. But I had never guessed how powerful her will was, how steely her control of herself.

"But about Harry ... Does anybody else know?"

I shrugged.

"I didn't *know* anything myself until the two of you admitted it all. But Walter told me about her having been hit on the head and I knew I was on the right road. Then it came to me what that thing was"—I pointed at the tail of the china dog—"and it all fell into place sort of at one time. I was only guessing, but it fitted with all the things that had never made sense about Dolly. The only thing that could explain her was Harry."

The last words were hard to force out. Each of them weighed a ton, and when I was rid of them my whole body felt drained and empty.

"Walter," Ellen said. "What else does Walter know?" The tip of her tongue showed nervously over her lower lip.

"Nothing but what I told you," I said. "Nothing he could prove, even if he wanted to. You won't have to kill him. He thinks the two of you are worth protecting, anyway."

She nodded calmly. "Then that just leaves you."

"Ellen …" Harry's voice was thin but steady. "Ellen, we can't go on doing these things, you know."

"Nonsense." She spoke as if it were all a matter of common sense, of which Harry obviously had very little. "There isn't anything else to do, just like the other time."

"Tell me about that," I said.

I had had a sudden notion. Maybe it was not worth much, but all I had started with had been another notion. Maybe this one would pan out too. Maybe I was even getting psychic; perhaps I would be able to come back from the dead and tell all.

"No," Ellen said. "Why do you—"

"Shut up." It was the first time I had ever heard Harry's voice or anyone else's actually force her into silence. It was as if, having made his last effort, having absorbed his final rejection, he was no longer subject to the ordinary pressures. He put his big hands back on the desk and began to toy with the tail of the china dog. He spoke to it, without looking at either of us.

It had been obvious, he said, as soon as he and Ellen had their wits together that night—and what he left unsaid here, what he passed over with a grunt, must have been so full of the agonies of whatever shameful truce they had had to make that even Ellen winced visibly—as soon as they had their wits together they had known they would have to think of a way to cover up what had been done. A fake suicide had been out of the question because who would commit suicide by hitting the back of her own head? An accident had been the only course left, Harry said, and Ellen had suggested an automobile accident. It had been her idea to run Dolly's Jaguar into the big boulder down the road. So between them they had carried her limp little body out to the Jaguar.

Here he paused and grunted again, in that same indrawn manner, as if the actual details of this act were unbearable, as if they had gone out of his mind and left a merciful blank. Ellen had said her nerves were steadier than his and she would drive it—and Dolly—down to the boulder. Harry had followed in his Cadillac.

Steady nerves or not, he said, it had been Ellen that had made both mistakes. First, she had parked the Jaguar right at the boulder, almost touching it. Second, she had parked it with the two left-hand wheels on the soft shoulder.

But they had not at first noticed either of these things, Harry said. Ellen had backed the car far away from the boulder and got it started going forward again along the flat dark road ... faster, faster, faster, until at last, with the manual throttle pulled all the way back and the powerful hand-built engine roaring hellishly in the predawn quiet, Ellen had leaped from the running board and rolled over and over and into the cotton field bordering the road. Just as she had scrambled herself to a halt the whole night exploded. The thing was done.

Except, as they had looked at the incredibly twisted and ruined pile of metal, the first pale hints of dawn had streaked the sky and they had begun to be able to see. They had seen where

Ellen had parked the Jaguar originally and where she had backed far down the road and where it had come roaring forward toward the boulder. It had all been there in those tracks, the whole story. In that gray dismal dawn they had looked at each other with the profound and terrible dismay of the wicked about to be made not only to pay for their sins, but to face them as well. It had even been too late to remedy anything, because just then they had heard an automobile approaching, a long way off, and all they had been able to do was get in the waiting Cadillac and speed away, miserable and afraid.

Except that self-preservation is a powerful urge, Harry said, and by the time they had reached Old Hundred, by way of several back roads, they had seen quite clearly that what they had actually done after all was to stage not a fake accident, but a fake suicide. And they had just had time to enter Dolly's room, type out a logical note on her portable, and go shivering to their own beds before the Sheriff had arrived with what he thought was tragic news.

"But we won't have that much trouble with you," Ellen said. "We won't have any trouble with you at all."

"Do you really think you won't?" I said.

"Of course." She smiled, showing her even white teeth, the corners of her red lips going up beautifully toward two spots of color high on her cheeks. "Everybody knows you've been crazy. That you've acted oddly here. That you assaulted Joe this morning. Who's going to question it if I say you came in here and attacked Harry and I had to shoot you to save him? Who's going to question Ellen Thompson if she says that?"

I wished Peggy would play again. Any sound at all would have been welcome. I thought desperately that if I shouted, perhaps someone would come to investigate; but shouting would not have stopped Ellen from shooting me, instead would have lent credence to her story that I had gone berserk.

"Now, listen," I said, speaking desperately against time, trying mightily to shape the notion flitting at the edge of my brain into a full-fledged idea. "You can't possibly—"

"Be quiet," Ellen said. "Stand over there by the window. Get out of the way, Harry."

My knees creaked and clicked like an old man's. It was a long shaky walk around Harry's desk to the window. He sat quite still until I was past, then got out of his chair and went to stand beside Ellen. She had not moved from the sofa, but the pistol had followed me carefully.

I was standing on a white throw rug. It was soft and pleasant under my tired feet, but it would not do much to break my fall after the shot.

"Ellen," Harry said, "do you know what you're doing?"

She was beautiful when she smiled. Her whole face changed and became softer and more pliable, as if it were actually made of flesh through which human blood moved. Seen above the black ring of the pistol muzzle, that slow lovely softening was blood-curdling.

"Of course I do. There isn't anything else for us to do, is there?"

But I would bleed all over the rug, I thought fantastically. I would turn it red with blood and ….

My head snapped up. The notion that had hovered just outside my mind had entered it full-blown and without argument I accepted it and began to turn it into a weapon. It was not much— little more than another guess—but it was all I had.

"Was there a lot of blood, Harry?"

His brows drew together.

"You mean here or … or out there?"

"Out there. After you ran the car into the boulder."

Ellen's breath began to hiss. All along my body, the skin began to crawl and tighten and tingle.

"What difference does that make? I don't even want to think about it any more."

"That's one of the reasons you don't, isn't it? Because it was so gruesome. Because there was so much blood."

"Sure, there was a lot of blood. It almost made me sick, there was so much of it."

"That's strange," I said. "Very, very strange."

"Harry, I'm sick and tired of his talking and talking and—"

"What's strange about it?" Harry said.

"Didn't you say Ellen killed her here with the china dog?"

"That's right."

"Dead bodies don't bleed," I said.

"Don't bleed?" Harry said. "But there was so much blood. It was all over everything."

"Of course there was blood," Ellen said. "There was bound to be blood, the shape she was in. You know there had to—"

Harry said, "But it was *flowing.* I saw it flowing and then ... it stopped ... while I watched."

"That doesn't mean—"

Harry's body moved in two directions at once; he stepped away from Ellen as if she were repulsive, and his arm streaked at her and he slapped her once, twice, back and forth across her face.

"She was *alive* when you ran the car into the rock!"

"No! No! Harry!"

He hit her again. The sound was as sharp and flat as the explosion of the firecrackers that had awakened me that morning to the Fourth of July. I edged around the desk toward them.

"She was alive and you *knew* it. You knew we didn't have to cover up any murder, but you went on—you killed her anyway!"

Ellen had thrust herself far back on the sofa, her legs drawn up as if there were snakes on the floor, her head held at an odd angle toward her shoulder. The pistol pointed only generally in my direction and she was not looking at me at all.

"She could still be alive. Dolly could be *alive!*"

I wanted to jump for the pistol, but Harry stood between Ellen and me. I could only stand and listen to the bleat of her voice:

"Don't you see, with her alive, it would have happened again! They'd have found out about you and her, Harry, they always find out those things, and they'd have laughed at us and pointed at us and we wouldn't have been *above* them any more!"

The muscles of his shoulders bunched and his arm went up over his head, the hand at the end of it clenched into a club. I watched the great arc of that club going down down down until it smashed into her face with the sound of a melon splitting in the sun.

She went over on her side on the sofa. I had one quick glimpse of that ruined face, bloodless no longer; then it was gone beneath those long white fragile hands. Her legs drew spasmodically against her and her skirt dragged far up over her knees and white thighs and the pistol fell behind them to the brown leather of the sofa.

"We didn't have to do anything," Harry said. "She could still be alive."

I lunged against him, driving my shoulder into his ribs. He staggered across the front of his desk and against the huge globe. It tottered and went over and he barely held himself upright by clutching the leather chair. I picked up the pistol from between Ellen's legs and stepped out into the center of the room, holding it loosely at my side.

"I never wanted to kill Dolly," Harry said. "Frank, you know I didn't."

My finger tightened on the trigger; only some powerful last vestige of civilization saved me from shooting him on the spot.

"Oh, yes," I said. "It was Ellen that had all the ideas, wasn't it? It was Ellen that knew what would happen if the two of you let Dolly live, too."

His mouth worked as if he were going to burst into tears. He leaned like a broken tree against his desk.

"But let me ask you this, Harry, this one thing: If you had known Dolly was alive in that car, do you really think you would have stopped it?"

Then, when we needed nothing but silence, Peggy started to play again. She swung into "Darktown Strutters' Ball" with a ferocity that almost passed for sensitivity to its dark rhythms. She played so loudly that she might have been in the same room with us. The pounding bass and rollicking melody were ghastly and vulgar in the quiet musty den where old Josephus looked down on what was left of his long distinguished line.

"Because Ellen was right. You'd have wanted Dolly again if she had lived. You'd never have got out of it any other way, Harry. It was either give her up or—sooner or later—give up this." I swept my hand around toward the constricting book-lined walls.

"I'd have stopped it," Harry said. "I loved Dolly."

"You don't know what the word means. In a way, I'm glad Dolly never lived to see you truly. It would have been like seeing the end of the world."

His shoulders squared a little and he drew a deep breath.

"I'd have stopped it," he said. "But I guess you have to think that. What are you … going to do?"

Through the gruesome swing of "Darktown Strutters' Ball" I heard Ellen groaning and snuffling into the leather of the couch. Here was the goddess, the high priestess, in all the panoply of her triumph. Dolly was dead and no one would ever know of the smirch. No one would ever be able to use these sordid grounds for not looking up to the Thompsons. The creed was safe, the faith protected, no matter what the cost.

"I'll leave that to you," I said.

"I'm going to divorce her," Harry said. "I'm going to throw her out, physically if I have to, and divorce her. She'll never tell any of it, anyway. She'll try to hold on to everything she can for herself."

I looked down at Ellen again. She had suffered the final indignity: Her hair had come loose and straggled about her smashed face. And it had all been for nothing. She had not saved herself after all.

"It won't be much," Harry said. "There won't be much left for her if she loses Old Hundred."

"Suit yourself," I said. "I wash my hands of her."

"And what about me?"

I put the gun in my pocket, went to the desk, and picked up the tail of the china dog. Then I walked to the door and unlocked it.

"I'll leave that to you, too," I said.

I had one last glimpse of Harry, head down, unmoving, contemplating, perhaps, what the future held. It must have been a chilling vision. It would have been much kinder to hit him or shoot him or even to turn him over to the police. He would have been glad to confess. For the rest of his life he would seek someone to confess to, so that he might also find someone to forgive him.

But I didn't feel kind. Something had driven Harry and Dolly and Ellen to all that they had done. All right. Let him take the consequences, too, as well as they. Let that same inexplicable human spirit which had ruined him tax him with the costs. It was creator and destroyer and avenger all in one. It was indestructible, too, and he was only beginning to feel its power.

In the narrowing crack of the door, I saw him for the last time. Beyond and above him, looking, at last, not so much powerful and forbidding as petulant and disappointed, the dark portrait of old Josephus looked down in perpetual disapproval.

I went upstairs, took a shower, and changed clothes. Then I went to the kitchen and had Easter fix me a ham sandwich. It was thick and dry but it filled up the void in my stomach. P.B. came in while I was eating. I told him I thought dinner was going to be a little late, thanked Easter for the sandwich, and went out the back door.

I walked a few steps from the house, took the pistol from my pocket, and threw it away. Then I went around the corner of the house toward the terrace. Maggie and Walter were sitting quietly in deck chairs, side by side, and George and Joe were playing cribbage in the light from the sitting room. Peggy was standing in the door. They were all drinking Martinis.

I walked past George and Joe into the middle of the terrace. No one looked surprised to see me. Somehow, I had expected them all to gasp or jump to their feet.

"I think dinner's going to be a little late," I said. "Harry and Ellen had a little ... dispute. They're kind of upset."

"Dispute?" Peggy said. "What about? They never fuss. What did Harry do to her?"

"What it amounts to is that I'm leaving right away."

It was quiet on the terrace. The bullfrogs were croaking on the other side of the house and a small breeze sifted the leaves of the two oaks on the lawn. Nobody said anything for a minute. There was a movement at the far edge of the terrace and Ann stepped across the faint boundary of light.

"Oh," Peggy said. "Oh, I see. You're leaving."

I didn't want to talk to Ann yet. I certainly didn't want to talk to Peggy. I went over to Walter and Maggie. Walter winked at me.

"You guessed right," I said. "I'll go along with you, too, but not for your reasons."

"What?" Maggie thrust her tanned face up at me. "What do you mean by that, Frank? Why do you have to leave?"

Walter lit a match and held it to his pipe. By its light, I could see the bland confidence of his face.

"People have to go on living," he said. "They can't undo what's done, can they?"

"You're damn right they can't." I looked out across the dark lawns to the yellow lights of Mack Norton's house, beyond Harry's meadow. They looked warm and bright and cheerful. I wanted to throw a rock at them.

"What?" Maggie was insistent. "What on earth are you two talking about?"

"Now, sweet," Walter said, "keep your blouse on, will you? All I'm saying, Frank, is you have to be careful about blaming people for things maybe they didn't have any control over."

I looked away from Mack's lights and past Maggie's upturned tanned curious face to the fat pipe in Walter's mouth.

"I don't blame anybody. But I hold them responsible, Walter. I have to do that and it doesn't have anything to do with blame."

"Frank?" Peggy said, behind me. I had the feeling that she was about to tug at my shirttail. "Should I go to Ellen, do you think?"

"What good do you think you could do *her?*"

"Well … I thought …"

"You leave her to Harry."

She pouted and went across the terrace to sit on the arm of George's chair. That was a good place for her but I didn't think she'd stay there. Walter put another match to his pipe. In its yellow glow, his face was still bland and confident and complacent.

"I don't understand this at all," Maggie said. "Why don't you tell me what's going on, Walter?"

"I will, sweet. Later." He held out his hand. "So long, Frank."

I took it briefly. "See you around, Walter."

I turned away.

"Frank," Maggie called. "Frank, don't you dare leave till you've—"

"Hey," George said. "Hey, Frank, you aren't leaving town, are you?"

I didn't answer George either. What was there to say? I looked for Ann but she had left the terrace. I turned away and went toward the sitting room.

"Hey," George called again, "we never got around to that bridge game, Frank."

I went into the living room, where the great piano that Paderewski had played stood mutely in the corner. It was best to break clean, I thought; it was best not to have any farewells with these people. Ever since I had come to Huntsville, I had knuckled under, not so much to them as to their composite idea of themselves. For their approval, I had been willing to deny the dignity of my own existence; I had tacitly agreed that they were a breed apart, a blooded cult capable of producing their own gods. And in the long run they were only human beings whose whole conception of the world and life and themselves was ludicrous. Their gods were not only false, they were not even grand, not even persuasive. It had taken me too damned long to learn that.

Out in the hall, P.B. was placing a vase of flowers on a table beneath the mirror. I surprised him. His startled face looked like that of an underfed monkey.

"P.B.," I said, "go upstairs and throw my things in my suitcase and bring it down."

He went up the stairs speedily, vastly relieved, I was sure, to have me going.

"Frank?"

Joe stood in the hall behind me, his hands in his pockets.

"I didn't want you to get away before—I mean, hell, I guess the fight was as much my fault as it was yours."

I had almost forgotten the fight. It seemed a lifetime ago. He swallowed and his cheeks sucked in, making his lean huntsman's face cadaverous. He blinked in embarrassment.

"A man ought not to lose his temper like I did, Frank. But ... hell, I had a right to love her, too."

Sure, I thought. You had a right to your version of Dolly just the way I had a right to mine. Maybe Harry had a right to his version, too. What difference does it make which version was right or if any of them was? None of them saved her.

I held out my right hand and he took it. He had a good strong grip.

"So long, Joe."

He held my hand a moment longer and went back toward the terrace. I heard George call out something to him but I couldn't make out the words.

High heels clicked down the stairs and Ann appeared on the landing. She was carrying a week-end bag. She hesitated, then came halfway down the rest of the stairs.

"Can I go with you, Frank?"

I stepped over to the stairs and put my hand on the polished newel post. She came down another step or two.

"You're jumping to conclusions, aren't you, Ann?"

"I don't think so."

It was crazy; or maybe it wasn't so crazy. I hadn't had time to think about it. Or maybe I didn't need any. I didn't know.

"I think it's a pretty good bet," Ann said.

She was wearing a straight plain dress of some light material; she looked small and desperate and hopeful and afraid. Right then, I wanted to go far away and find a place where there was no one at all. But there was no such place. And, even if there were, I knew I would not always want to stay there; sooner or later, a man always tires of being alone.

And I had found her, anyway; somehow I had pierced her anonymity and given her an identity of her own. There was where I had failed Dolly. She had come to me, too, in search of an identity, and I had failed to give it to her, had failed to understand that what was needed was not my entry into her world, but hers into mine. I couldn't undo that, but I didn't have to repeat it.

"You'll have to learn to like fishing," I said.

"If you want me to, I'll learn to like bricklaying."

"I'm going to be a long way from here. A hell of a long way."

She came all the way down the stairs and I put my arm around her waist. There was no stiffening, no drawing away.

"There's nothing to keep me," she said. "Not any more."

I pulled her close to me. It was going to be all right, I thought. It was going to be fine.

Over her shoulder I saw P.B. come down the stairs carrying my suitcase. The lines creasing his monkey-like face were deep and stark. Behind him, the grandfather clock began to chime, just as it had every hour for more than a century.

"Let's get out of here," I said.

I slept for a long time after we drove away from Old Hundred. When I woke up it was almost midnight and we were still going. I didn't know where. I didn't care, either.

Too late, I remembered that I had not even noticed when we had passed the rock. I had not even read the straggly letters across its face. "REPENT," they would have said if I had seen them. But I couldn't repent. I had to believe that Dolly had found what she really wanted. I had to believe that she had died in full flower, in the final realization of herself. I had to believe that her version of Dolly was the most accurate of all.

I had to believe all that instead of repenting. I rolled down the car window and the night air came in fresh and vital on my face. I leaned out and threw the tail of the china dog as far as I could.

"What was that?" Ann said.

I slid across the seat and kissed her cheek. It was warm and sweet-tasting.

"Something I didn't want any more," I said.

THE END

www.ingramcontent.com/pod-product-compliance
Lightning Source LLC
Chambersburg PA
CBHW022157240626
47153CB00007B/2710